THE ASCENT OF D.13

An exciting story of cliff-hanging suspense in its most literal sense...

The newest, most secret weapon was tested over an airfield in Germany, by an RAF plane which was then ordered to land in Cyprus. On the way the plane was hijacked and course set for Russia, but it crashed in mountains close to an international frontier between East and West. The wreck containing the vital equipment lay in fog, snow and blizzards at 13,000 feet. A team of professional climbers is assembled to make the ascent of a major peak, under dramatic conditions and political pressure – and to make the return journey...

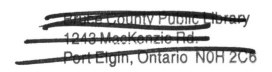

THE ASCENT OF D.13

by

Andrew Garve

Dales Large Print Books
Long Preston, North Yorkshire,
BD23 4ND, England.

British Library Cataloguing in Publication Data.

Garve, Andrew
    The ascent of D.13.

    A catalogue record of this book is
    available from the British Library

    ISBN   1-84262-450-4 pbk

First published in Great Britain in 1969 by Collins

Copyright © Andrew Garve, 1969

Cover illustration © Len Thurston by arrangement with
P.W.A. International Ltd.

The moral right of the author has been asserted

Published in Large Print 2006 by arrangement with
Andrew Garve, care of Curtis Brown

Dales Large Print is an imprint of Library Magna Books Ltd.

Printed and bound in Great Britain by
T.J. (International) Ltd., Cornwall, PL28 8RW

CHAPTER I

THE CRASH

The aircraft circled the proving ground at twelve hundred feet, its twin turbojet engines throttled well back. It was an ageing British fighter-bomber which had been taken off the strength and converted to new uses. Its bomb-bays were empty; its guns and rockets, radar and reconnaissance cameras had been removed. A bulkhead, put in to enclose the nose for some earlier experiment, had been left in place, but the rest of the interior had been stripped right down so that the crew could move around more freely. At the moment, the plane was being used as a flying test bed. It had R.A.F. markings, a British pilot, an American navigator and radio officer, and a civilian German boffin for the special job in hand. Because of the joint nature of the enterprise, the NATO top brass had decided it would be tactful to have a mixed crew.

The pilot, George Crale, was a Cumberland man, thirty years old, with a face as craggy as the fells that had bred him. He had been hand-picked for the job because of an outstanding flying record and long experience with fighter-bombers. He was in his ejection seat on the port side of the forward fuselage, under a bubble-type canopy that gave him an excellent field of view ahead, above, and on both sides. He was watching with fascination the preparations on the ground, and waiting for instructions from Control.

The navigator, Eddie Paton, was a Texan from El Paso. He was twenty-eight, no more than averagely tall, but very powerfully built. He was seated at his table right forward beyond the bulkhead with his back against the starboard wall of the fuselage. As he had no navigating duties to perform at present, he also was watching the ground scene with interest, through the plane's transparent nose.

The radio operator, Steve Lowe, was a fresh-faced, crew-cut youngster in his early twenties, a southerner from Atlanta. He was sitting beside his W/T instruments half-way along the fuselage, watching with lively curiosity the activities of Peter Frankel, the German boffin.

Frankel was a man who normally would have been quite out of place in a fighter-bomber. He was middle-aged, balding, spectacled and podgy. He was kneeling on the floor, fiddling lovingly with the red-painted box-of-tricks in the belly of the plane

6

which was what the day's experiment was all about.

As the aircraft started on its sixth circuit, Crale put the port wing down a little to give himself a wider view of the proving ground. He saw below him a wood of tall trees, still leafless in early March; some low, camouflaged buildings, well dispersed among the trees; a large, grassy field, winter-bleached and criss-crossed by vehicle tracks, with traces of old snow under the hedges; and an artificial lake with a ribbon of white road running beside it. From its general appearance, the place could have been anywhere in north western Europe – but in fact it was a few miles from Frankfurt, in Germany.

All around the ground there were scenes of intense activity. A column of marching troops was just emerging from the wood. A Centurion tank was lumbering round the edge of the field and another, smaller, one was describing a figure of eight in the centre. Boats of various types and sizes were manoeuvring on the lake. A convoy of half-tracks, lorries and guns was rolling along the white road.

Crale continued to circle, holding his height. Below, the scene slowly changed. The column of troops marched back into the wood. The tanks left the field and took cover in the trees. The boats made for the lake shore and concealed themselves under bushes. The convoy of vehicles turned off the road and laagered in a quarry.

Crale's headphones crackled. 'Zeta calling O for Orange,' an American voice said. 'Okay, we're ready. Make a double run at a thousand.'

Crale acknowledged, and called across to the boffin. 'We're going in, Frankel.' The German looked up and nodded. Crale brought the plane round in a wide sweep, lined it up on the centre of the field, put the nose down and eased the power, and levelled off at a thousand feet, watching his radio altimeter. Frankel concentrated on the sights and press buttons of his box-of-tricks. The field, the lake and the wood flashed by. Beyond the proving ground, Crale banked and turned and did a careful run back at the same altitude.

'Fine,' came the voice from the ground. 'Now at five hundred, both ways.'

'Going in at five hundred,' Crale said. He brought the plane round again, losing height, levelling off meticulously, and made his second double run. As he cleared the wood for the last time the boffin straightened up and gave Crale the thumbs-up sign. 'Excellent!' he said.

Crale reported to the ground.

'Right,' came the voice, 'that's all, then. Happy landings.'

Crale acknowledged, and took the plane up to five thousand feet and called Base. 'This is O for Orange reporting mission at Zeta completed.'

'Thank you, O for Orange. You're cleared for Cyprus. Have a good trip.'

Crale muted the R/T and turned the plane to the south. With luck, he thought, they ought to have an extremely good trip. A thousand miles of fine weather, a swim in the Med., a beer or two, and a lazy evening before the next set of trials. Just the ticket.

He called the navigator on the intercom. 'What did you think of it, Eddie?'

'My, it sure is scary,' Paton said.

'Yes – hard to believe, isn't it...? Right – what's the course?'

'A hundred and ninety-three magnetic,' Paton told him.

'Roger.'

Crale set the autopilot and went aft to the toilet.

When he emerged, he could hardly believe what he saw. Lowe, pale and scared, was backed up against the forward bulkhead with his hands half raised. The boffin was pointing a gun at him. As Crale appeared, the gun swivelled. 'Stay where you are, Crale. One move towards me and I shoot.' Frankel's accent was guttural, his English fluent. 'Lowe, go into the nose.'

Crale stared into the barrel of the Luger, then up at the boffin's face, incredulously. 'Have you gone nuts, Frankel?'

'By no means,' Frankel said.

'Then what's the idea?'

'Our destination has changed. We are going east.'

'East...?' For a moment, Crale didn't get it.

'To Russia,' Frankel said.

Crale's eyes dropped to the red box – and all was clear. 'Why, you lousy...!'

'Save your breath, Crale... Lowe, into the nose!'

Crale stood motionless, measuring the distance that a rush would have to carry him. About eight feet. A couple of seconds. It was tempting. Frankel, forty and flabby, would be easy meat at close quarters. As he obviously knew. Sweat glistened on his high forehead. He wasn't as cool as he sounded. Probably an amateur gunman. All the same, the Luger was steady, the fat forefinger crooked in a businesslike way round the trigger. And a bullet would take less than two seconds...

Crale said, 'Suppose you do shoot? You think you can land this plane on your own?'

Frankel shook his head. 'That would be impossible. But I have faced all the consequences. I am committed now – I have no choice but to go on. If necessary, I am prepared to crash.'

Crale could believe him. The man was clearly a fanatic – and desperate. He'd shoot, all right. And at eight feet, he could hardly miss. No point in risking it – not yet...

Crale spoke to Lowe. 'You'd better go, Steve. See you later.'

For a moment, Lowe hesitated. Then he nodded, and went through into the nose, closing the door behind him.

Frankel motioned with the gun. 'Get into your seat, Crale.'

Crale went forward. Frankel leaned back against the ribs of the plane, tracking him with the Luger as he passed. Crale took his seat under the canopy and flicked on the R/T. As he'd expected, it was dead. So was the intercom. He glanced back at the W/T set, and saw wire hanging loose. The plane could fly, but its crew were out of touch with each other and the world.

'Climb to ten thousand feet,' Frankel said. 'Change course to ninety-five degrees magnetic. Your speed will be five hundred knots.'

Crale cut out the autopilot, pushed on more power and put the nose up. At eight thousand feet the plane ran into thick cloud. At ten thousand Crale levelled off. The radio altimeter was still working. Frankel's sabotage had been skilfully selective. Trust a boffin...

The German came nearer, glanced at the compass and the air speed indicator, saw the course was ninety-five and the speed five hundred, and gave a satisfied grunt. 'That is good. I am glad you have decided to be sensible.'

'Where are we heading for?' Crale asked.

'Volgograd,' Frankel said.

'Volgograd! That's a hell of a long way. What's wrong with just over the border?'

'The weather is very bad in western Russia,' Frankel said. 'The cloud is almost down to the ground, and there is much snow.'

'In that case we've a good chance of getting lost.'

Frankel shook his head. 'We shall be tracked by Soviet radar all the way. When the weather clears, as it will towards the end of our journey, we shall be met and escorted in. It is all arranged. There will be no difficulty.'

'You must have been keeping in very close touch with your friends.'

'Yes – right up to this morning.'

Crale grunted, and fell silent. For a while the only sound in the plane was the whine of the engines. Then he said, 'What I don't understand is why the Russians need to have the actual box. You know what's in it – you could have told them how to build it.'

'I know only a part,' Frankel said. 'There were many of us working on it, and the secrets were divided.'

'I see... I suppose you've been planning this for a long time?'

'I have been hoping for an opportunity ever since I joined the unit,' Frankel said. 'To-day, through a fortunate set of circumstances, it came.'

Crale nodded slowly. From the boffin's point of view, the circumstances had indeed been fortunate. Anyone from the unit might have got the proving assignment – but Frankel had got it. The plane, on any other day, could have been light on fuel – but its tanks had been filled for the long trip to Cyprus, as Frankel, of course, had known. And now, because of the opaque cloud cover, interception from the ground was impossible. No doubt the West Germans below were calling the unidentified plane, tracking it, and wondering what the hell it was up to. But there was nothing they could do about it, short of shooting it down. Nothing anyone could do about it – except the crew themselves...

Crale put in the autopilot and sat back, concentrating on the problem of how to get the gun from Frankel. He thought he could see a way, if things worked out right. The boffin might know a lot about electronics and lenses and infra-red rays but he didn't know much about fighter-bombers. It should be possible to catch him off balance, some time in the next three hours – perhaps when he was tiring a little, when his guard was lowered. It was just a question of waiting for the right moment, and being ready for it when it came.

The attempt would have to be a co-operative one, of course. Crale couldn't work it alone – he'd need to stay in his seat. And it would be up to the others to initiate the action. Without the intercom, Crale couldn't even drop them a hint. But Eddie and Steve, so quiet in the nose, were certainly not sitting and twiddling their thumbs. Crale had flown enough hours with them to know their calibre. At this very moment they were probably working out some plan – and their thinking was likely to be along much the same lines as his own. They could be trusted to make the right move – when conditions seemed favourable.

Crale switched his thoughts to the problem of what he'd do *after* they'd got the gun…

There was very little talk between the two men during the first hour. The German had no fresh instructions to give, and Crale had nothing useful to say. Argument, he knew, would get him nowhere, and abuse would be positively dangerous. Frankel must be lulled, not provoked. The one exchange Crale started was designed to suggest resignation over the turn of events.

'Do you think your friends will let us go back to Germany after we've landed?' he asked.

'Of course,' Frankel said. 'It is the box they are interested in, not you.'

Crale gave a sigh of satisfaction. 'Well, that's something.' He hoped his relief sounded genuine. Privately, he thought it most unlikely that the Russians would be prepared to admit that one of their agents had hi-jacked a NATO plane. They'd try to cover up somehow. And if they denied the hi-jacking, obviously they wouldn't be able to return the crew. On Crale's reckoning, it was the Luger or a labour camp. Or worse…

The interior of the plane had darkened. Crale switched on the lights and checked his watch against the clock on the instrument panel, 14.50 hours. They'd been flying at five hundred knots for more than ninety minutes. By now they must be far into Russia.

Frankel had been right about the weather. The cloud mass had thickened over Poland, and snow had begun to fall. The air was getting bumpier. Strong beam gusts were shaking the plane. Pockets opened above and below it. There was the familiar upward surge, the moment of suspension, the sickening drop. The staggering and shuddering.

Crale was used to it, but he'd never liked it. Who could? At any other time he'd have taken the plane up to look for something better. Not this time, though. Probably he wouldn't have been allowed to, anyway – but

15

he was careful not to suggest it. For once, it suited him to be thrown about. He guessed it would be suiting Eddie and Steve, too.

He glanced round at the boffin. Frankel was leaning back against the starboard side of the aircraft, six feet away from Crale. He'd been standing like that for most of the trip, so he could keep his eye on the compass and the speed indicator. Silently watching, with the Luger always at the ready.

He looked strained and tired, which was hardly surprising. Definitely not as alert as he had been. And decidedly green around the gills. Crale turned up the heat control, just to make things a bit more uncomfortable for him. And to give Eddie and Steve the only sort of signal he could.

It was a few minutes after 15.00 hours when the door in the forward bulkhead opened a fraction and Paton cautiously stuck his head out.

Frankel swivelled the gun. 'What do you want?' His tone was sharp.

'It's hot as hell in here,' Paton said. 'You trying to fry us, George?'

'Sorry,' Crale said, and turned the heat down again.

Paton eased himself through the door. 'We need liquid, Frankel – we're seizing up. You must be pretty dry, too. How about some coffee?'

Frankel's tongue licked over his lips. 'Where is the coffee?' he asked.

'In the locker by the can. Two large flasks.'

Frankel hesitated. He needed liquid more than anyone – the tension of the flight had parched him like a desert. 'All right,' he said, after a moment. 'But keep well away from me as you pass. If you make the slightest move in my direction I shall at once shoot you in the stomach.'

'Don't worry, bud,' Paton said. 'I'm not arguing with a gun. All I want is coffee.' He came out, hands in the air, looking at Crale. The message in his eyes was that there was a message. Crale read it loud and clear. He dipped the port wing, just enough to rock the plane. Paton gave the faintest nod and moved on, keeping well over to the port side of the fuselage. He passed Frankel at eight feet, nervously eyeing the Luger which was pointing at his navel. He reached the locker, and took out a bulging bag.

'Slide it along the floor to me,' Frankel said. 'And stay where you are.'

Paton slid the bag to the German. Frankel took out one of the flasks and a packet of sandwiches, and shot the bag along towards the bulkhead. 'All right,' he said. 'Back you come, my friend – but be very careful. Give some refreshment to Crale, and return at once to the nose.'

Paton started to go forward, his right hand

17

above his head, his left clutching the ribs of the plane to steady himself against the bucketing. Frankel leaned back against the starboard wall, covering him with the gun as he advanced. Paton's face was tense. He was almost level with the German. He was watching Crale.

Crale was watching him. *Now....!* He rammed on full power and turned the fighter-bomber on its port wing tip. Paton jerked backwards, out of the way, his body hard against the ribs. Frankel shot across the plane and crashed down on the almost horizontal port wall. Before he could recover, Paton was on him. There was almost no struggle. In a moment he had snatched the Luger from the bruised and winded boffin.

Crale levelled off the aircraft. 'Nice work, Eddie,' he said. 'Very nicely timed.'

The crew were together in the cockpit. Frankel had been disposed of, dumped in the toilet with his feet and hands tied to keep him from further mischief. Lowe had taken a look at the damaged radio instruments and reported that it would be half a day at least before he could get them back in working order. The plane was on autopilot, still at ten thousand feet. Snow was no longer clogging the canopy, but the cloud outside was as thick as ever.

Crale said, 'Right, Eddie – where do you

reckon we are?'

Paton pulled a face. 'Are you kidding? The last fix I got was when we left Zeta, and I'm not clairvoyant... Did we do five hundred at ninety-five all the way?'

'Yes,' Crale said.

'Then let's see...' Paton spread out his track sheet, drew a line, looked at his watch, pencilled in a little square and wrote the time beside it – 15.35 hours. 'By dead reckoning,' he said, 'we're there.'

Crale studied the sheet. 'Say a hundred miles west of Volgograd.'

Paton nodded. 'Give or take fifty square miles.'

'How's the fuel?' Lowe asked.

Crale glanced at his gauges. 'We've a safe ninety minutes' flying time at five hundred knots. More if we throttle down a bit.'

'Is that enough to get us back into friendly territory?'

'Yes, if we fly south over the Caucasus,' Crale said. 'Turkey's a NATO country, and we should be able to make it with something to spare.' He re-set the autopilot on a provisional 180 magnetic while they went on talking.

'It'll be dark in a couple of hours,' Paton said, 'and we've no radio aids. Where will you put her down?'

'I haven't a clue, Eddie. We may have to bale out.'

19

'That'll be jolly.'

'Better than life in a salt mine,' Crale said.

'Oh, sure… What are the Russians going to do about us in the meantime?'

Crale shrugged. 'Your guess is as good as mine. They'll know something's gone wrong, if they're tracking us, but they won't know what. We'll just have to keep our fingers crossed.'

'Mine are stuck that way,' Lowe said.

Crale was back in his seat, and had control. Airspeed was four hundred knots, to economise fuel; course 176 magnetic, height twenty thousand feet to clear the mountains. The cloud was getting wispy, but visibility through the canopy was still virtually nil.

Paton was thumbing through some typed sheets. 'There's an air base at a place called Kars,' he said, 'just over the border. But heaven knows how we'll find it.'

'We'll find it if the Turks start shooting at us,' Crale said grimly. 'Let's hope they decide we're friendly.'

Lowe swallowed some coffee. 'They'll need to be mind-readers,' he said.

Silence fell for a while. The aircraft raced on through the gloom. Crale was watching his gauges. He had just over thirty minutes of flying time left.

The interior of the plane began to grow lighter. At last they were coming out of the overcast. Suddenly the cloud broke, and there was clear sky ahead. An evening sky, with dusk not far away.

Crale dipped the nose and gazed anxiously down. All he could see was range after range of snow-covered mountain tops, desolate as a moonscape. The echo of the radio altimeter gave him four thousand feet to the summits. He went down two thousand for a closer look. A few lights, widely scattered, were beginning to twinkle in the valleys. By dead reckoning, the plane was close to the border – but where in that frozen waste the border ran was anyone's guess. And as for a landing place…!

'It looks as though we will have to bale out,' Crale said. 'But we'll fly on as long as we can. We don't want to finish up in Russia after all this.'

'You're dead right, we don't,' Paton said.

'Will you get the chutes, Eddie?'

'Okay… How about Frankel? There's one for him, but he won't know how to use it.'

'We'll put him in my seat and tell him how to eject,' Crale said. 'He'll have more chance that way. I'll use his chute… Better get him untied.'

Paton nodded. 'I hope that guy lives. I'd like to see him in the dock some place.' He went off to get the parachutes.

Lowe said, 'Why the hell don't the Turks come up and lead us in, now it's clear? We

21

could still make it.'

Crale said nothing. He was searching around for some sign of a town, even a village. An inhabited place they could drop near and hope to survive. But the mountains looked fiercer and emptier than ever. And only fifteen minutes to go...

Suddenly, as he gazed ahead, a bright object flashed past the nose. He caught its markings – a red star on the fuselage. 'God, that was a Mig!' he cried.

A moment later the fighter-bomber was raked with bullets. Holes opened in the sides. Lowe slumped silently to the floor. Paton staggered in through the bulkhead door, blood streaming from his neck, and collapsed gurgling beside the cockpit. There was a thump and a bang at the rear of the plane – a cannon shot hitting the tail, Crale guessed. He wrestled with the controls. Hopeless! The tail had gone. The plane was plummeting. There was nothing he could do to save it now. He glanced round at his crew. Both men were dead or unconscious. He couldn't save them, either. This was it. He put his hands behind his head and pulled down the cowl of his ejection seat. The seat did the rest.

CHAPTER II

THE ASSAULT

Royce showed out the newspaper reporter from the *Cumhuriyet* who had been interviewing him in his hotel room over breakfast, made sure he had enough Turkish money for the day, stuffed a street plan of the city in his pocket, and prepared to leave for his first look at Ankara in daylight. He had reached the door when the phone rang. It was Tommy Garson, telephoning from the British Embassy. Garson was the Counsellor there. 'Morning, Bill,' he said. 'How about a nice drive?'

Royce smiled. 'Not for me, thanks!' He and Garson had arrived in the Turkish capital late the previous night after an arduous twelve-day journey overland from London in a Ford van. 'I'm going to spend the day standing up.'

'Fine!' Garson said. 'Come and stand up at a cocktail party here this evening. H.E. wants to show you off to the colony. Good for the British image and all that. Proof we're not decadent.'

'Oh, lord!'

'It's the price of fame, old boy – you can't

duck it. Okay?'

'All right, Tommy, I'll be there. It's extremely civil of him, of course, I appreciate that... How's work going down?'

'I've forgotten I ever had a leave,' Garson said. 'See you around six, then. 'Bye.'

Royce took the van across to a garage opposite the hotel and arranged for it to be washed and serviced. Then, with the street map in his hand, he started to walk. He was a well-proportioned man of medium height, sinewy and supple, with the easy carriage of an athlete in good trim. After the long sessions in the Ford, walking was a sensual pleasure. The March weather was cold – a degree or so below freezing – and fresh snow creaked under foot. In Ankara, on the high Anatolian plateau, winter had still a long way to go. But the air was dry and crisp, and the sun was shining, and altogether it was a splendid day for exploring.

Royce, when the mood was on him, was an insatiable sightseer. He didn't at all care for crowds and noise, and half his life was spent in some of the loneliest spots on earth. Yet, for a spell, any city of character could draw him like a magnet. He had enjoyed every minute of his brief stopover with Garson in Istanbul, marching up and down its seven hills and taking in the ancient monuments with shameless speed. The huge, squat pile of St Sophia, which he'd thought impressive even if it was a lifeless museum now; the Suleiman Mosque, graceful and compelling in its imperial splendour; the fascinating Seraglio Palace on its wooded promontory. Where else in Europe was there anything comparable? He had gazed down with delight from Camlica Hill on the panorama of the Sea of Marmora, and the Bosphorus, and the Golden Horn crowded with caiques. He had even spent an hour in the teeming labyrinth of the old town, squalid though it was. Istanbul might lack charm, but it was uniquely stimulating and it positively reeked of history.

He had enjoyed, too, in a different way, the day-long drive over the new highway from Istanbul to Ankara, which Garson had thought dreary – the steep climb on to the plateau from the coast; the treeless, barren waste, flecked with snow, that stretched as far as the eye could see; the occasional village tucked away in a ravine on the side of some eroded hill; the white-capped mountain summits in the distance. There hadn't been much life around at this harsh season of the year, but there'd been plenty of landscape. And landscape was one of Royce's passions.

He spent only a little time in Ataturk Boulevard, the main street and traffic channel that cut through the Turkish capital from end to end. It was busy, thriving and cosmopolitan, crowded with businessmen and officials and foreign diplomats and smart Turkish army officers and American G.I.'s; and noisy with the babel of a dozen different tongues. With its luxury shops and great hotels, its rectangular office and apartment blocks, its government buildings and banks and travel agencies, it seemed to Royce to offer neither more nor less than the centre of any other capital city, and he didn't tarry.

Instead, he made his way on foot to the old town, attracted by its position on a huge, sand-coloured rock and its romantic silhouette against the cold blue sky. He spent a zestful hour there, exploring its fort and its patched ramparts, poking amongst stone blocks and fallen columns, turning over bits of rubble to examine Greek and Roman decorations, pausing to decipher a little of Augustus's life story inscribed on the wall of a marble temple. Afterwards he wandered though the maze of cobbled alleys, peering into dark cafés where old men squatted over hubble-bubbles and young men played cards, admiring the carpets and oriental silks and metal work on display in the tiny shops, marvelling at the great loads carried by trousered women through the tortuous lanes, and delighting in the brilliance of their colourful head-scarves and shawls and dresses.

He descended the rock in time to lunch at

a small *lokanta*, on watermelon, *shish kebab* and yoghurt. While he sipped his coffee he had his shoes cleaned by a swarthy youth who chewed pumpkin seeds and chattered to him in film American. Then he joined a *dolmus*, the communal Turkish taxi, for the experience; and had himself driven up to the yellow stone pile of the Ataturk Mausoleum, not least because he'd been told it commanded a superb view of the city in its amphitheatre of hills. As he gazed out across the snowy rim he had the feeling that some day he'd like to come back to Turkey, in the early summer, when the flowers were out and the earth was tawny. It was a country that deserved more than a cursory glance on a winter's day.

At four o'clock, replete with new sights and pleasantly exercised, he returned to his hotel to dress for the embassy party.

'Come along and meet H.E.,' Tommy Garson said. He was plump and rosy-cheeked, a well-grown cherub, with twinkling eyes and a lot of social charm.

He took Royce's elbow and steered him through the crowd towards a tall figure who had just detached himself from a group. The bibulous party chatter quietened momentarily. Heads turned, and whispers of recognition followed Royce as he edged his way forward. He tried to look unconcerned, without wholly succeeding. He was still not quite used to being a celebrity.

The ambassador caught sight of them, and closed the gap. He was a big man with a handsome, rubicund face and a slightly amused expression, as though he had just heard a scandalous piece of gossip and would have loved to tell it but knew he mustn't.

Garson said, 'I'd like to present Bill Royce, sir. Bill – Sir John Avery.'

The ambassador shook hands warmly. 'Welcome to Ankara, Mr Royce. It's good of you to join us.'

'A pleasure, sir.'

'Thomas tells me you had quite a rough trip.'

'Rough!' Garson said. 'My rump feels as though it's been bastinadoed.'

Royce smiled. 'It was a bit rugged in places – though we expected it at this time of year, of course. The worst section was between Belgrade and Skopje – deep potholes and washouts for miles, and a lot of mud and soft snow. We were stuck for hours.'

'What was the object of the exercise?' Avery asked. 'Enjoyment, or mortification of the flesh?'

'Neither, Sir John, as a matter of fact. I had to bring out most of the gear for the expedition – practically everything except boots – and I thought it would be cheaper by van than by sea, and almost as quick. The

28

fact that Tommy was returning from leave fitted in very well for both of us.'

'I don't doubt *he* was glad to hitch a ride... So what are your plans now?'

'Well,' Royce said, 'Bob Everett's flying in from Mombasa in about a week and he and I will take the van on to India by easy stages. Pearce and Carruthers expect to join us at Manali at the end of April. We should be in the Chandra valley by mid-May, at the start of the season, and we'll be climbing for about six weeks.'

'More virgin peaks?' Avery asked.

'I hope so – there are still plenty of them about in the Himalaya. But mainly we're planning to attack the north face of Nangenjunga if the weather's good.'

'That sounds formidable. Will you be sending your usual pieces to *The Times?*'

'Yes, if I can get them through.'

'Then I must try and keep track of you... So you expect to be here for some days. Do you know Turkey at all?'

'No – this is my first visit.'

'How did you like Istanbul?'

'I thought it was fascinating.'

Avery nodded. 'Turkey's a fascinating country. When people discover it, it's going to have a great future as a tourist centre. Freya Stark called it "the most splendid, varied and interesting country in the world," and I'm inclined to agree with her. It has beauty, colour, an excellent climate in the south, blue seas, fine beaches – and a wealth of archaeological treasures... Are you interested in ancient monuments, Mr Royce?'

'Very much so,' Royce said.

'Well, Turkey's got more ruins than Greece – though unfortunately they're not all so accessible. But the place is opening up fast – wherever you look there are new roads, new airports, new hotels. The Americans are pouring money in. A lot of it is going on military aid, of course – building up the NATO bastion – but not all, by any means. They're doing a tremendous job in helping to modernise the place.'

'I noticed there were a great many Americans in the town,' Royce said.

'Oh, you'll see them everywhere – servicemen and civilians. They're building airfields and hydroelectric stations, deepening harbours, exploring for oil and minerals, making social surveys – all with their usual drive...' Avery broke off. 'Well, I mustn't monopolise you any longer. Perhaps you'd care to dine with us one evening if you're not too busy – my wife's in Izmir but she'll be back to-morrow and I know she'll be most disappointed if she doesn't see you before you leave.'

'That's very kind of you,' Royce said.

'You're at the Kara Palace, aren't you? I'll get my secretary to ring you in the morning... By the way, if you're keen enough on monuments to make a trip, and have a day to spare, I strongly recommend a visit to the Hittite reliefs at Konya – they're extremely fine... Now let me introduce you to some of your fellow guests.'

'Enjoy yourself,' Garson murmured. 'I'll see you later.'

Royce did his conscientious best as the lion of the party, shaking hands affably with all comers, answering the same questions over and over again, being charming to diplomats and officials and their wives, sidestepping invitations without discourtesy, and generally putting on a good show. But he found the din and the hot, smoky atmosphere hard to take, and as soon as the gathering began to thin out he made his excuses and withdrew thankfully to his hotel. He dined there in blissful solitude, and shortly after ten o'clock he went up to his room and turned in.

He slept well, till the telephone rang by his bed. He fumbled for the receiver, drowsily, and switched on the light. 'Yes...?'

'Bill!' The voice was Garson's, unusually sharp. 'Will you come over to the embassy?

Royce looked at his watch. It was five o'clock. 'What – *now?*' he said in astonishment.

'Right away – it's an emergency. I'm sorry – I can't tell you anything more on the phone. A car will be round to pick you up in ten minutes.'

'Okay,' Royce said. He hung up, and started to dress. By the time the phone rang again to say the car was there, he was ready.

2

The embassy forecourt was choked with vehicles. Several of them had U.S. Army or U.S. Air Force markings; one belonged to the Turkish Air Force, one had the insignia of the Turkish Foreign Ministry. A conference was evidently under way, and a pretty high-powered one if the transport was anything to go by. Royce went quickly into the vestibule, wondering if war had broken out. A servant took his coat and showed him into the spacious room where the cocktail party had been held. A dozen men, some in resplendent uniforms, some in civvies, were standing around in small groups, talking earnestly in several varieties of English. The ambassador was there, immaculate and urbane in spite of the hour, looking as though he was rather enjoying the flap. Garson was with him, and one or two more of the embassy staff whom Royce had met during the evening. The others were strangers. As Royce went in, the buzz of conversation stopped and everyone turned, as though with relief. It was apparent that they'd all been waiting for his arrival.

The ambassador approached, and greeted him. 'I do apologise for bringing you out at this ungodly hour,' he said. 'You'll hear why it was necessary in a moment... First, let me introduce these gentlemen. Mr Kilchuk, of the Turkish Foreign Ministry. Air Marshal Omer, Turkish Air Force. General Hassan, Turkish Army. Colonel Salem, Turkish Security. General Burns, United States Army and Supreme Allied Command, Europe. General Lawson, U.S. Air Force. Captain Gene Brogan, U.S. Army. The others I think you know. Right – let's pull up chairs and get to business.'

There was a brief pause while the company arranged itself in a half-circle. Then Avery said, 'General Burns, would you care to start the ball rolling?'

'Sure.' The general leaned forward, addressing himself to Royce. He was a grey-haired man in his middle fifties, authoritative and very distinguished-looking. 'I'd like to say first, Mr Royce, that all of us here are familiar with your great record and achievements and we're honoured to have you with us.'

There was a murmur of assent from the company, and Royce inclined his head in acknowledgement.

'Now let me put you in the picture,' Burns continued. 'On the morning of the 7th of March – that's the day before yesterday – a NATO aircraft with a secret device on board was hi-jacked while it was flying over Germany, and taken at gunpoint into Russia. It had almost reached Volgograd, its intended destination, when the crew succeeded in disarming the gunman and regaining control. The pilot didn't have sufficient fuel to fly back to Germany, so he made for Turkey, the nearest friendly country. Just short of the border the Russians shot the plane down – obviously in a last desperate attempt to keep the device inside their own frontiers... Of course, the Russkies don't admit any of this. The version they put out yesterday was that an American plane had invaded their air space, run into bad weather, and crashed in flames at an unspecified point. They've had the gall to lodge an official complaint in Washington! Anyway – to get back to facts – the pilot, a Britisher named Crale, managed to bale out. The rest of the crew, and the German Commie who did the hi-jacking for the Russians, are presumed dead. The pilot was lucky. He not only landed just inside Turkey – he touched down within a couple of hundred yards of a Turkish frontier post. He sustained a broken arm and slight head injuries, but he was able to talk. That's how we know what happened.'

The general paused for a moment to light a cigarette, then continued. 'Naturally our first concern was to find out where the plane had crashed, and whether there was anything left of it. A Turkish reconnaissance aircraft flew along the frontier yesterday morning and, just north of where Crale landed, it located and photographed the wreck. The plane had dived into snow and hadn't caught fire. It's pretty well broken up, but the fuselage appears to be more or less intact – so the device may be intact, too. The plane came down, Mr Royce, on top of a mountain peak which stands exactly on the border between Turkey and Soviet Armenia.'

'Ah!' Royce said, seeing a gleam of light.

'We can safely assume,' Burns went on, 'that the Russians also succeeded in locating it yesterday – and considering the efforts they've already made to get this secret, we can assume as well that they'll attempt to reach the wreck and remove the device. What we don't know is how much of a hurry they'll be in. That depends on whether or not they believe we're still in the dark about the fate of the lost plane. When the pilot baled out it was getting on for dusk, so the Mig that shot him down may not have spotted him. Our reconnaissance plane would have been tracked by Russian radar, but by a fortunate chance yesterday was the day of its regular frontier patrol, so the Russians would have had no reason to connect its flight with the crash. On the other hand, they might have supposed it would have spotted the wreck, even if it wasn't looking for it. In all these respects, we're just guessing. The only safe assumption to make is that the Russians know we know, and that they'll get to the scene as fast as they can. And we've got to beat them to it. That, Mr Royce, is why you've been called in. You're a mountaineering expert, and we need your advice and help.'

'In what way?' Royce asked.

'The mountain will have to be climbed, Mr Royce. In other conditions we'd have sent a helicopter up and landed a party on the summit. So, no doubt, would the Russians. But an hour or two after yesterday's reconnaissance, the weather deteriorated. The mountain tops are in cloud – a slow-moving belt of cloud that extends for hundreds of miles. The Met. people say there'll be no change in the situation for five or six days at the earliest – and until there is, no helicopter can operate usefully or safely at summit levels. So the wreck can only be reached on foot. Mr Garson here tells us you have all your climbing equipment with you – and there's no doubt you have the know-how. What we want to ask you, Mr Royce, is whether you would be willing to lead a two-man party – yourself and another man, that is – up the mountain, in an effort to forestall the Russians.'

'I see…' Royce was silent for a moment. Then he said, 'Could I have a look at the reconnaissance picture?'

The Turkish Air Marshal, Omer, delved in

a briefcase and produced a photograph and a map of the area, both of which he passed to Royce.

Royce looked first at the photograph. It showed a waste of high, snow-covered ground, with what appeared to be a mountain ridge running through its centre. A section of the ridge had been ringed in red. Inside the ring, Royce could just make out some dark shapes in the snow. One of them looked like the detached fuselage of an aircraft and another like a piece of broken wing, and there were various smaller bits of debris dotted around. The picture showed little else of interest. It had been taken in dull weather, and from too great a height to give any useful impression of the mountain's contours.

'Is the wreck on Turkish soil or on Russian?' Royce asked.

Kilchuk, the Foreign Ministry man, said quickly, 'It is quite definitely on Turkish soil, Mr Royce. If that were not the case, we should not be able to agree to the suggested action. The frontier there runs along the highest part of the mountain ridge. At the point where the plane has fallen, our maps show that the highest ground is at the extreme northern end of the ridge, after which it drops precipitously. So, since the wreck is on the ridge, it must be in Turkey.'

'Not that that's likely to bother the Russians too much,' Burns put in drily. 'If they find they've got the summit to themselves when they get there, it's a fair bet they'll go right ahead and do what they want.'

'Is the frontier marked physically on the mountain?' Royce asked. 'Are there any border posts? Any cairns? Any wire?'

'There is nothing,' Kilchuck said. 'Elsewhere the Russians have taken the utmost precautions, constructing a fence along the whole of their six hundred kilometre frontier with my country and setting up watchtowers at frequent intervals. But at this point they evidently decided that the task was too great, and that Nature was sufficient. Their wire stops at precipices on either side of the mountain.'

Royce nodded, and opened out the map – a large-scale military sheet, with coloured contours. The site of the plane had been marked by a small red cross, just south of the dotted frontier line. The place where it lay was slightly to the east of the mountain's actual summit, and a few hundred feet lower.

'There's something printed here that looks like "D.13",' Royce said. 'What does that signify?'

'It is our designation of the peak,' Omer told him. 'The mountain has no name. D is for *dag* – the Turkish word for "mountain".'

'Ah, yes...' Royce studied the contours. 'According to this, the summit's around four thousand metres – something over twelve thousand feet. That would mean a long approach climb if one had to do the whole of it – but I see that the peak rises from very high ground all around.'

Omer nodded. 'That is so, Mr Royce – and it is fairly accessible ground. If the cloud base remains where it is, we should be able to set you down with your equipment at perhaps three thousand metres. It is the last thousand metres that would be your problem.'

Royce could see that. The faces below the summit were very steep on all sides – almost sheer walls, he guessed, from the solid massing of the contours. It was hardly surprising that the Russians hadn't troubled to run wire over the top.

'What would be the height of the permanent snow line in those parts?' he asked.

'I would think,' Omer said, 'a little over three thousand metres.'

'Is it an area that gets a lot of snow?'

'Yes, very deep snow in most winters. And this one has been no exception.'

'What sort of temperatures are usual there in March?'

'They can go very low indeed – perhaps twenty degrees of frost Centigrade at night. But with the present overcast, it would be much warmer.'

'Yes, of course... By the way, has the mountain ever been climbed from this side?'

'Not to my knowledge,' Omer said.

'Have you any close-up pictures of it?'

'I think not.'

'So virtually nothing is known about it at all?'

'That is true.'

Royce turned again to Burns. 'If I agreed to undertake this trip, who would go with me?'

The other American general, Lawson, said a little diffidently, 'Well, Mr Royce, if there'd been time we'd have asked you to suggest someone yourself, someone who already had your confidence, and we'd have flown him in. But there isn't time – if we're going to beat the Russians to the top we've got to start moving right away... Apart from yourself, we believe Captain Brogan here is the only man on the spot who is capable of tackling the job. If you're agreeable, he'll accompany you.'

Royce looked carefully at Brogan. He was a man of about Royce's own age, but taller, broader in the shoulders, altogether heftier. His hands, Royce noted, were big and muscular. His eyes, in a tanned face, were flinty grey and his jaw line was rugged. Royce had the impression of a pretty determined character.

'What do *you* think of the proposition, Captain?'

'Tough,' Brogan said. 'Mighty tough.'

Royce nodded. 'Would you care to tell me about yourself? As a climber, I mean.'

40

'Sure,' Brogan said. 'I'm not making any big claims. I don't pretend to be in your class, Mr Royce, and I've never hit the headlines. I guess I never will. But I've been climbing ever since I was a kid, in all weathers and conditions. I've been a member of some fairly strenuous expeditions – the last one was up the southeast spur of Mount Mc-Kinley, though we didn't quite make it. I've done more Very Severes than I can remember. I'm sound on rock, and I'm pretty good on ice and snow. I know all the technical tricks and I won't need teaching. Where you can lead, I reckon I can follow.'

Royce gave a noncommittal nod, and for a while studied the map again. 'Well – this isn't an easy decision to make…'

Burns said, with a touch of anxiety, 'Maybe it would help, Mr Royce, if I were to tell you just how much depends on this device.'

'Not the fate of the world, I hope!' Royce said gravely.

'Not quite that, maybe – but a lot of lives could depend on it. The details are classified of course, but I'll tell you as much about it as the Russians know… The device is a kind of camera that looks back in time. It uses an infra-red process to take crude photographs of things that have happened in the past, by registering infinitely small amounts of heat. The basic research was done in the States but a German unit came up with a greatly refined

41

process, which is why the lost plane was mainly operating in Germany. The camera is still in an experimental stage, but we've great hopes of it. If it comes up to its promise, it could mean that an aircraft was able to photograph the movements of troops and guns and trucks on the ground some time after they'd passed by. It could put an end to secret concentrations by night and maybe change the whole course of warfare in jungle territory. That's how important it is.'

'It sounds fascinating,' Royce said. 'And how much does this piece of apparatus weigh?'

Burns frowned. 'I wouldn't know exactly. I'd guess around a hundred and twenty pounds.'

Royce stared at him. 'Surely you're not suggesting that two of us could get that down a mountain like D.13 in winter, in addition to all our other equipment?'

'Indeed I'm not, Mr Royce. We don't expect to get the camera back. It happens to be one of several we've built, and our pro-gramme can go ahead without it. What we're chiefly concerned about is to deny it to the Russians. Once they know how it works they'll be able to take counter-measures, and it'll have lost its value... No, the idea would be to destroy it. Captain Brogan would take some explosive with him and blow it up where it lies.'

'I see...' Royce pondered. 'What if we ran into the Russians while we were up there?'

'The aim would be to avoid that,' Burns said. 'It's true you'd be on a legitimate job, with right on your side, but up there in the wilds with nothing to mark the border the Russkies might be prepared to argue the point – and with so much at stake they could get rough. Your plan would be to move fast, get there first and in secret, carry out the demolition before they could intervene, and withdraw without a confrontation. The last thing any of us wants is a scrap on the frontier.'

Kilchuk nodded vigorously. 'That is most important, Mr Royce. We do not wish our relations with the Soviet Union to be impaired by this unfortunate happening. There must be great discretion and no incidents.'

There was another pause. Then Royce said, 'How would we get to the mountain?'

'You would be flown from here to Kars in a Turkish aircraft,' Omer told him. 'From there, a helicopter would take you as near to the peak as the weather conditions allowed. With luck, to the foot of the south face.'

'When is it suggested we start?'

'As soon as you can get your gear together,' Burns said. 'The whole thing turns on speed. If you could leave for Kars this afternoon, you could be at the face and ready to begin your climb by dawn to-morrow. I doubt if the

Russians will be able to beat that. They'll have their own problems of organisation and transport, maybe worse than ours, and they don't move that fast – except in space!'

'What would be the arrangements for getting us back?'

Omer said, 'If by any chance the weather cleared in the next few days, we would send a helicopter over the summit and locate you and lift you off when you gave the signal. If, as is more likely, conditions remained bad, the helicopter would keep a daily watch on the lower slopes of the south face and pick you up when you had completed your descent. You can rely on us to maintain the closest contact with you that circumstances permit.'

Royce nodded, and sat in silence, weighing things up. His thoughts were almost solely on the technical feasibility of the climb. At this stage, with so little information available, the difficulties were hardly calculable – but they would certainly be enormous. The mountain face would be treacherous with snow and ice – and not just a light winter mantle. The fact that the summit was well above the permanent snow line would probably mean there'd be glaciers and ice falls and crevasses to negotiate towards the top. Royce doubted if anyone in that room, except Brogan, had the least conception of the fierce struggle the assault would involve. Or the dangers. Two on a rope, though fine for speed and mobility, would leave little margin for error or accident. And to undertake such an expedition with an untried companion was, by normal standards, lunacy. If Brogan turned out to be less than first-class, they wouldn't have a hope. All the same...

Burns broke in on his thoughts. 'Well, Mr Royce – what's your verdict?'

'The ascent may prove impossible,' Royce said. 'There can be absolutely no guarantee of success. But it's an exciting challenge and I'm willing to have a try. How about you, Captain?'

Brogan grinned. 'I've no option, Mr Royce. I'm under orders.'

3

The main conference had broken up, with a final, cautionary word from Burns on the importance of maintaining secrecy about the expedition. Outside in the forecourt, quiet discussions were still going on around the cars. Brogan appeared to be getting some additional instructions from the American brass hats. Royce called to him that he was going to collect the van and would be back in half an hour, and got a lift to his hotel. He left word at the desk there that he was going off on a sightseeing tour for a few days, asked

45

them to hold his mail, and arranged to retain his room. He snatched a cup of coffee, made out some lists, and by eight-thirty was back at the embassy with the van. The last of the cars was just leaving. Royce parked the van in a quiet bit of drive behind the building, where he could sort out his equipment away from prying eyes, and Brogan joined him there for a planning session.

'How long a trip are we reckoning on, Chief?' Brogan asked.

Royce had already given some thought to that. 'On past experience,' he said, 'I think our absolute maximum will be five days on the mountain. We oughtn't to try and hump loads of more than about fifty-five pounds each, including climbing equipment – and with all the gear we'll need to take, we shan't be able to carry more than five days' food and fuel.'

Brogan nodded. 'That's about what I figured. Anyway, if we can't make it in five days I guess we shan't make it at all… What food are we taking?'

'If you're agreeable,' Royce said, 'we'll use some of the daily rations I had packaged up in England – it'll save us quite a bit of shopping time. Here's what's in them.' He gave Brogan a slip of paper. 'It's supposed to be a balanced diet. It allows us just over two pounds a day each.'

'That should keep us slim.' Brogan ran his

eye down the items. Coffee and tea, sugar, biscuits, oatmeal, concentrated meat bar, dried milk, egg and vegetable, cheese, butter, jam, chocolate and sweets. 'Yeah, that's okay with me – if I can add a few packets of gum... What sort of cooker?'

'A petrol pressure stove,' Royce said. 'Light and clean.'

'Uh huh... How much fuel?'

'Two pints.'

'That should be enough. What about rope?'

'I suggest two hundred and fifty feet of nylon medium, to use doubled for climbing and single in case we have to rope down a long way. And a hundred and fifty feet each of nylon full as a spare.'

'I agree with that,' Brogan said. 'Better to have too much than too little.' He looked inside the tight-packed van. 'You're going to have a job choosing what you need from all this stuff, aren't you? Anything I can do to help?'

'I don't think so, Captain. It's not as chaotic as it looks.'

'Okay – then I'll leave you to get on with the countdown and go and get my own gear.'

'Here's a list of what I'll be taking,' Royce said. 'It'll save you duplicating unnecessarily.'

'Thanks.' Brogan pocketed the list and climbed into his army jeep. 'I'll be back well before blast-off. See you!' He shot away in a spray of gravel.

As soon as he'd gone Royce started to sort out the contents of the van, discarding and selecting for the particular job ahead, and methodically checking everything against his list. He'd made these trip preparations so often that he knew the basic inventory almost by heart, but it was never safe to rely on memory. A single oversight could spell disaster in a crisis. As he checked, he spread the gear out on the ground. Rucksack, boots, ice-axe and crampons. Lengths of rope, carefully measured, with the necessary slings. Outer and inner clothing, for the worst conditions they were likely to meet. Too much of it, probably, but cold could be the deadliest enemy... Bivouac sack and two-man tent. Cooking utensils, specially chosen for lightness. Stove and fuel. Ten rations of food. Selection of hardware – pitons, rings, hammer. First-aid kit. Snow goggles. Lightweight binoculars, and compass. And all the smaller things... A pocket torch. Candles. Matches in a waterproof tin. Whistle, knife, string, map...

He rejected, after some consideration, the protective plastic helmets with built-in lamps that he'd brought for the Himalaya climbing. There shouldn't be much danger from falling stones on this trip if the sun wasn't going to show at all – and night climbing with lamps would be hopeless in cloud. He rejected too, reluctantly, the air beds that could make such a difference to comfort at night. They weighed too much. Some other form of insulation would have to serve...

He had almost reached the end of the list when Garson emerged from the back of the embassy and joined him. 'How are you getting on, Bill?'

'Pretty well,' Royce said.

'The Turkish Air Marshal just phoned through. He suggests laying on a plane at three. Think you can make it?'

'Just about.'

'Good – I'll let him know.' Garson gazed down at the piles of gear. 'Heavens, you're not going to tote all that stuff up the mountain, are you?'

'Can't avoid it, I'm afraid. It's the minimum.'

Garson picked up a crampon, thumbing the sharp steel points. 'I assume this goes over a boot.'

'That's right. It gives you a grip on ice and snow.'

'What are those iron pegs for?'

'They're pitons. You drive them into cracks in the rock and anchor yourself to them... The snap rings are for linking the rope to the piton, or one rope to another.'

'And these rope loops?'

'They're called Prusik slings. They're to

49

help you climb out of a crevasse if you fall in.'

Garson shook his head. 'Rather you than me, old boy, that's all I can say. I'd be frightened to death.'

Royce laughed. 'Well, don't let it depress you. I'd make a lousy diplomat.'

Brogan returned in the jeep just before noon. He had stowed his equipment loosely in the back, under a rug. As he removed the cover Royce sauntered across and ran an appraising eye over the gear.

'I see you've given up nails, too,' he said. Brogan's climbing boots were of the same post-war pattern as his own, with vulcanised rubber soles.

Brogan nodded. 'I reckon these grip better in most conditions – certainly on clean rock and sloping holds. Maybe they're not as good as nails on iced rock, but you can always use crampons.'

'I agree,' Royce said. He examined Brogan's rucksack, noting the broad leather straps at the shoulders, the capacious side pockets, the waterproof lining that could be drawn tight at the mouth. He fingered Brogan's bivouac sack, mitts and gloves, and his windproof smock. They were all of good material and right for the job. He tried Brogan's ice-axe, cutting an imaginary step with one hand. 'Nice balance,' he said. He felt reassured. The fact that a man had well-chosen equipment didn't necessarily mean he was a good climber, but it pointed in the right direction. 'Where's the explosive you're going to use?'

'In the sack.'

'What is it – dynamite?'

'Holy smoke, no! – not where there's risk of a fall. It's plastic.' Brogan groped in the rucksack and produced a small parcel, which he unwrapped. It contained a lump of what looked like light brown clay. It was pliable, with the texture and something of the smell of marzipan. 'Ideal stuff for cloak-and-dagger work,' Brogan said. 'It'll stand any amount of rough handling, it doesn't deteriorate and it isn't affected by weather. And a detonator goes into it like a knife into butter. You simply trail a wire, get out of range, and give it a shock from a small battery – and wham!'

'Have you got all those things?' Royce asked. 'Wire, battery, detonator?'

'Sure – in here.' Brogan opened one of the side pockets of the rucksack. A metallic barrel gleamed.

Royce said, 'What's the gun for?'

'Just a precaution. Wolves, bears – you never know.'

'Bears hibernate in winter,' Royce said.

Brogan grinned. 'Some of them do, bud. Russian bears don't.'

51

4

They were packed and ready to leave by three o'clock. They said good-bye to the ambassador and Garson in the privacy of the embassy and departed in an atmosphere of stealth. An official Turkish car with discreet markings collected them at the door and swept them quickly to the airport, entering through a side gate with only a cursory check from the guard and depositing them close beside the steps of the special plane that had been laid on for them. By three forty-five they were airborne in clear weather, only a little behind schedule.

As the plane gained height and turned east on its five hundred mile journey, both men relaxed. Whatever problems and responsibilities might lie ahead of them on the mountain, for the next fifteen hours or so they would be in the hands of the plain clothes security officer who was accompanying them to Kars. He was a large and impressive Turk named Enver, a man of great courtesy and dignity, with a fluent command of English. He had the permits that would allow them to enter what was normally a forbidden military zone, and the authority to deal effectively with any local difficulties. Royce had the feeling that if he had been wearing a uniform, it would have had a lot of shoulder stars and quite a few ribbons.

At the moment, having seen his protégés comfortably settled in the spacious cabin, Enver was up in the cockpit with the Turkish crew. For the first time Royce found himself alone with Brogan in leisurely privacy and it seemed a good opportunity to learn a little more about him.

'Have you been stationed in Turkey long, Captain?' he asked.

'About three years,' Brogan told him.

'You're an expert on something, I imagine. What do you do?'

'I was a hydraulics engineer back home, before I joined the army. Right now, I'm helping to build a dam up in the Taurus mountains.'

'Sounds a tough job.'

'I've no complaints. It's pretty rugged up on the site, but the work's interesting – and I reckon to get away most week-ends.'

'Where do you go?'

'Sometimes Istanbul, if I can hitch a ride in a plane. Sometimes Uludag – that's an army skiing centre near Bursa, up by the Sea of Marmora. Sometimes Ankara – specially in the late summer and fall. It's pretty nice then in the capital – kind of golden, and lively, with everyone out of doors and plenty to see. Screwy things, like a feller I once saw carrying a peacock up the main street – you'd never find that back home. And you get these guys, scribes they call them, like in the Bible, sitting out on the sidewalk opposite City Hall, writing petitions and letters for folk that can't do it themselves... I enjoy nosing around and watching what's going on.'

'Do you get any climbing?'

'Oh, sure. Mostly in the Taurus – nothing very ambitious, but enough to keep me in shape.'

'Who do you climb with?'

'There's another guy at the dam who comes along with me. He's raw, but keen, and I'm training him. Last summer I took a Turk up Mount Erciyas – that's the 13,000-footer that was called Argaeus in the old days. Now *there's* a climb I wouldn't recommend to anyone – boy, was it hard going! All lava and pumice chips and brittle rock.'

'Do the Turks go in much for climbing?'

Brogan shook his head. 'Only when the army makes them – this guy was an exception. Mind you, they could be damn' good at it if they wanted to – they've got plenty of nerve and they're nimble as goats – but they don't see any point in it. They reckon climbing a mountain just to get to the top is crazy.'

Royce smiled. 'They're not alone in that... How do you Americans get on with them, in general?'

'Pretty well,' Brogan said, 'especially at the higher levels. The G.I.'s have their troubles now and again – not taking the Moslem view of alcohol and women...! Me, I really go for the Turks. They've got their faults, like most people – they aren't always very efficient and they like to work in sudden bursts rather than steadily. Make you pretty mad sometimes. But they're a cheerful people, and courteous, and so hospitable it isn't true. Up at the dam, they'll bring you baskets of flowers and apricots and peaches in the summer, and they won't take a goddam cent in payment. What's more, they're good allies – tough, reliable. They've got sound ideas about the Commies over the border, and they don't change them – which is more than can be said for everyone...' Brogan looked as though it was only good manners that kept him from pursuing the theme. 'Tell me about yourself, Royce. Do you have a line, apart from climbing?'

'I used to teach history,' Royce said. 'I was a junior lecturer at Cambridge for a year or two. Now I just write the odd book – sometimes history, but mostly about mountains. It isn't a living, but I happened to be left a bit of money. Splendid for climbing – ruinous for steady work.'

'Lucky guy!' Brogan said. 'I wish somebody would ruin me with a bit of dough.'

The cockpit door opened and Enver came out. 'I thought you might care to know, gentlemen, that we are now flying over Sivas – the place where Kemal Ataturk, the founder of modern Turkey, raised his revolt in 1919.'

55

They looked out, dutifully, over the mosques and minarets of the town. The conversation switched to the Turkish revolution. It was some time before Enver returned to the cockpit.

Royce sat closer to the window and gazed down. They were flying now over high, rugged country, striped brown and white under a thin covering of snow. Paths were visible, scratched into the hillsides at unlikely angles, but there were very few roads. Only rarely did some movement catch the eye – a peasant on muleback, leading a line of donkeys; a caravan of camels; a sledge zigzagging down a dizzy track; a construction gang with a bulldozer; a military convoy; an infrequent rural bus. There were ruined buildings – an ancient fortress, a monastery, a chapel – but the only habitations were clusters of stone hovels in tiny villages. Almost the only vegetation was an occasional patch of withered scrub, bent by the tearing wind. Vein-like rivers, bridged with stone, twisted their way in deep gorges that scored the switchback folds of the plateau. Screes and precipices sliced up the tortured landscape.
'God, it's savage!' Royce said.
Brogan nodded. 'It gets a heck of a lot worse farther east.'
'You've been this way before?'
'Yeah – I had a spell near the border a

couple of years back, tapping underground water for a garrison post near Ararat. I wanted to climb the mountain – thought I'd check up on that story of Noah's Ark! But they wouldn't let me. The summit looks right down into the workers' paradise, and Big Brother's sensitive about folk peering over.'

'What time of year were you there?'

'Early summer. It was pretty pleasant then, except for the dust and flies. The grass and the flowers were so deep you could hardly see the animals. Takes a bit of believing now, but it's true... Interesting what was going on there – especially the nomad camps. Those guys live in goatskin tents with carpets on the ground and shut the women and kids away behind wicker screens and guard the camps with big yellow dogs that look like they'd tear your throat out... And around June all the villagers go up with their herds to the mountain pastures. Boy, do they have livestock! I never saw so many sheep and goats.'

'What happens in winter?'

'Most of the nomads go south, down towards the Med. The villagers go underground – they live in burrows in the slopes of the hills. It's so cold they have to. In January the thermometer there can get down to minus forty Fahrenheit. And in summer it can be over a hundred. What a range!'

Royce nodded. 'I believe it's supposed to be one of the biggest in the world.'

A movement on the ground caught Brogan's eye and he pointed down, enjoying now his role of guide. 'See those bullock carts? Well, you should hear them close to! The axles go round with the wheels and they squeal like crazy. I'm not kidding – it's enough to burst your drums. They say wives always know when their husbands are coming home because each cart has its own special squeal. Kind of useful for those that need an early warning…!'

He pointed again, as they flew over the flat mud roofs of a village. 'Now that's something else I learned – every one of those roofs has a round stone bar on the top for rolling the mud smooth after rain. Keeps the water out, I guess. They make the women do it…'

The talk died down after that. Royce continued to look out of the window. A tiny train was creeping up a valley, hauled by two ancient locomotives. It was the only sign of life. The country was getting wilder, the snow deeper, the villages more scattered. Even where there were habitations, no one moved outside them. The Turks, like the bears, seemed to be hibernating.

Presently the plane flew into cloud, the ground was blotted out, and Royce sat back. Brogan, he saw, had dozed off. Soon he was nodding, too.

He was wakened by sudden pressure in his ears. The plane was going down fast. He looked at his watch. It was almost half past five. The cloud around them began to thin, and in a moment the ground reappeared. They were over a town. Through the twilight gloom he could make out wide streets, a fortress above a gorge, a church with a red conical top. Lights were beginning to twinkle. Above the gorge, a tracery of electric lamps picked out the familiar profile of Ataturk. They had reached Kars.

Enver said, 'Follow me, gentlemen, please.' He led the way across the hard-packed snow to a small two-storeyed building of stuccoed brick that stood on its own at the edge of the airfield. It had the Turkish star and crescent illuminated above the entrance and a row of red-painted fire buckets beside the door. Somewhere at the back a radio was playing cheerful music. The air inside was warm, and smelt appetisingly of food. The building seemed to have no connection with the ordinary working of the airfield and Royce decided it must be some sort of guest-house.

Enver showed them into a large, carpeted room with wicker chairs and a wicker table. A chased silver samovar gleamed on a stand in a corner. Royce and Brogan dumped their sacks and took the seats that Enver offered them. Presently a Turkish servant came in and with a salaam to the guests began to serve glasses of tea and sweetmeats. He was a very spruce, elderly man with a white spade-shaped beard, brown face and beaked nose, and he was wearing a round grey cap and grey jacket, peach-coloured trousers and a double-breasted emerald waistcoat with a watch chain across it. His name, it appeared, was Ahmet. There seemed to be no one else in the house, and there were no indications that anyone else was expected. It looked, Royce thought, as though he and Brogan were to be kept incommunicado for the night.

While they sipped their tea, Enver outlined the arrangements for the morning. 'I shall be accompanying you as far as the mountain,' he said. 'It is about eighty kilometres from here, and the trip will take us about half an hour. We shall board the helicopter outside this building shortly before dawn. We shall fly as close as possible to the ground, and we shall approach the mountain by a route which will keep us well away from the frontier until we turn in for our landing. This, and the poor light, will make it difficult for the Russian frontier guards to study us closely, if at all. Once we reach the mountain we shall be hidden from them by the curve of the border, which turns a little to the north on both sides. Helicopter flights in the area are not at all unusual, so there is a very good chance we shall get through without attracting any special interest.'

'How about when Captain Brogan and I are climbing?' Royce asked. 'Will the Russians be able to see us then?'

'Not if you go straight up the mountain face from the south,' Enver said. 'If you move on to the east or west faces, you may well come into view. It is something to remember.'

Royce nodded. 'What exactly is the frontier set-up, Mr Enver? How is it guarded?'

'The Russians have watch towers at intervals of about five hundred metres,' Enver said. 'Boxes built up on girders, with observation platforms. The towers are linked by two rows of high wire fences, with bare ground between them which the guards inspect each morning for signs of footprints. At night, the whole length of the wire is illuminated by powerful lights.' Enver smiled wryly. 'Our great neighbour is much more concerned about the border than we are. On our side, we are content with a few boundary stones.'

'Does anyone ever get through?' Brogan asked.

'It happens from time to time, though usually elsewhere. There are always a few courageous and desperate men who will take any risk. There was one who swam for sixteen hours in the icy waters of the Black Sea to gain his freedom. But most of the Russians who come illicitly into our country slip away from Soviet ships in ports like

Istanbul, and hide in the bazaars till the danger of discovery has passed...' Enver made a deprecatory gesture, as though the subject were one he preferred not to pursue. 'Now, if you will excuse me, I will go and arrange about some food. You must eat well to-night, gentlemen – since it may be your last good meal for some days.'

The meal, when it came, was excellent. It began with several glasses of raki, the Turkish aniseed apéritif. There followed a delicious salad of tomatoes and cucumbers; marinated fish; tender spicy mutton with rice, served in dishes of hammered copper; and, at the end, a variety of preserved fruits. Royce and Brogan both did full justice to the repast. Afterwards the three men sat for an hour over cigarettes and sweet coffee, talking about Turkey and the problems of its eastern provinces.

'It must be pretty lonely for people serving in this part of the country,' Royce said.

'Indeed, yes,' Enver agreed. 'For many, especially those who are used to big cities like Istanbul and Ankara, it is a life of exile – a patriotic duty which they perform willingly, but with no great pleasure. The wives, in particular, have much to endure in our garrison outposts, where often the lodgings are poor, heating primitive, and there is little to occupy them. Sometimes, in a bad winter, they lack even the telephone. But all this will change in time...' He got up. 'Now, as we have to make an early start in the morning, I am sure you would like to rest...'

He took them upstairs to a simply furnished bedroom, with two single beds. 'We have, I am afraid, no running water in this house, but a supply has been brought up for you. I wish you both sound sleep. Ahmet will wake you at half-past four.'

In fact, they were wakened earlier – by the sound of the helicopter coming down outside the building. Ahmet arrived soon afterwards, bearing tea, girdle cakes and white cheese, which they ate without great appetite. Brogan stuck his head out of the window and reported that it had snowed a little during the night, that the temperature at a rough guess was three or four degrees below freezing, and that the cloud base seemed not to have changed. They dressed for the mountain, in light sweaters and windproof smocks and fingerless woollen mitts; pulled on their climbing boots, and joined Enver downstairs. As the first grey showed in the east the three men took their seats behind the Turkish pilot and co-pilot and the helicopter climbed away at a gentle angle, blowing a cloud of loose snow behind it in the rotor's slipstream.

Though they were flying low over the ground there was little to be seen in the pre-dawn murk, and what there was looked wholly uninviting – wild uplands bare of everything but snow, with here and there an icebound stream or frozen lake. Once they had left Kars behind, the Turkish border territory was empty. The only lights they saw came from the Russian frontier fence, coiling away round the contours like an illuminated snake. And they were far away.

The helicopter had been flying for twenty minutes when Enver suddenly pointed ahead. 'There is your mountain,' he said. To Royce and Brogan, the place he was pointing at seemed at first no more than a dark gap in the frontier lights. Then a shape began to emerge, a towering mass that rose abruptly from the plain, its summit lost in cloud. As they drew nearer, the frontier lights went out. The flight had been well-timed. Dawn was just breaking.

The pilot circled, looking for a safe place to land. Close to the mountain base there was a broad gully, flat at the bottom and only lightly covered with snow. He made a wide sweep, began a gently inclined descent, hovered for a moment over the gully, and set the helicopter down on its skids.

Brogan stood up and stretched. 'Well, we've made first base,' he said cheerfully. He opened the door and climbed down into the snow. Royce lowered the packs to him, and followed. Enver leaned out. 'Good luck, gentlemen!' he called. 'The pilot will keep a close watch for your return.'

The rotor turned faster, the helicopter lifted. Enver gave a final wave as it swung away. In a few moments it had disappeared into the gloom. Royce and Brogan were alone with their packs, in as desolate a spot as either of them had ever seen.

5

They walked up the side of the gully till they had an unobstructed view. Then Royce got out his binoculars and sat down on his rucksack to study the scene.

Ahead, for about three hundred yards, there was a smooth snow slope, steepening sharply near the foot of the mountain. From there the face rose precipitously to the cloud base two thousand feet up. Royce judged the average angle to be about eighty degrees. Much of the face was bare rock, but there were sizeable patches of snow and ice on ledges and in pockets. The summit, somewhere to the west, and the ridge that ran down from it – their ultimate objective – were hidden in cloud. Below ridge level, and well to the east, there appeared to be a cleft in the mountain. Much of it was obscured by a high shoulder, but Royce suspected a *couloir* and a glacier. He could see formidable amounts of snow and ice up there. However, that wouldn't concern them – at least for the moment. That was the side where they'd be visible to the Russian guards.

He turned the glasses on to the south face again, looking for possible routes. There was no way up that immediately suggested itself – no continuous fault, no easy and obvious path of ascent. He could see several cracks, vertical and slanting, but they were too widely separated to constitute a route.

'Just as we thought,' he said. 'It'll have to be by guess and by God.' He passed the glasses to Brogan.

Brogan made his own careful inspection. 'Yeah – that's a pretty intimidating sight.' He sounded more eager than intimidated. 'Okay – let's get cracking. Do we rope up here, or wait?'

'Might as well rope now,' Royce said.

They got out their waist cords, and climbing rope, and the crampons they'd need for the snow slope, and shouldered their sacks. Each had a share of the food – a precaution in case they were parted by some accident – and a selection of pitons and slings. Royce's load was the lighter, as he was to lead.

Out of the corner of an eye, Royce watched Brogan prepare himself, noting his technique. Separate waist loop, passed five or six times round the body outside the smock and tied with a reef knot. Free ends neatly tucked away. Snap link clipped on. Nylon climbing rope tied to snap link with Tarbuck knot.

Spare end of rope coiled in and slung across body over shoulder. Butterfly knot to snap link. All good standard practice... Satisfied, Royce concentrated on his own preparations.

The two men were ready within moments of each other. Brogan gave a final heave to his huge pack, settling it comfortably. 'I reckon we should have brought a small crane,' he said.

Royce smiled. 'Or one of those flying carpets the Turks go in for.'

'That's right...' Brogan picked up his ice axe. 'Okay, Chief – run out your string.'

Royce set off up the slope at an unhurried pace, bent forward a little under his load, his motion a slightly exaggerated walk as he raised his cramponed boots to clear the snow. Brogan followed in his footsteps, twenty feet behind. At first the surface was firm-packed snow that gave no trouble, but presently it changed to hard ice and the angle steepened. Royce swung off on a rising traverse, striking all ten points of his crampons strongly and precisely into the ice and balancing on bent ankles. When the slope grew steeper still he started to cut steps, two at a time, cracking the ice with the pick of his axe and then breaking out small chips for a step the size of his boot sole. At intervals of a few yards he waited, the spike of his axe driven well in against a slip, while Brogan came up with him. The last fifty feet to the face were covered in a zigzag that brought them to an almost level ice shelf below a promising crack in the rock.

They paused there, panting a little. At nine thousand feet the air wasn't all that thin, but they'd had no time to acclimatise and the angle had been sharp. Royce, in particular, was feeling the effects. He usually depended on an approach walk to the mountains to get climbing-fit. Instead, he'd been sitting for two weeks in a van. Still, a day or so would bring him back to form...

He looked up, scanning the rock face. There was an icy glaze on some of the surfaces that would be slippery in rubber soles. And there'd be ledges and holds covered with frozen and re-frozen snow. 'I shall keep my crampons on,' he said. Brogan nodded. 'I was figuring the same.' Royce parked his ice axe in the loops behind his rucksack and stood for a moment studying the crack, selecting his first holds. 'Right – let's see how it goes. You'd better anchor, Captain.'

Brogan glanced down the steep ice slope. 'I guess so.' He ran a loop from his waist over a spike of rock and tied it into the snap link with a butterfly knot. Then he passed the rope round the small of his back and held the slack in his feeding hand, ready to pay it out or to take any strain. Nothing could prevent it running out fast in the event of a fall, but a steady constant grip, a sliding arrest, could check the fall and prevent tension building up in the rope to snapping point... Royce, watching him, gave a nod of approval, and started to climb.

Except for the occasional icy surface, the first patch presented no difficulties. Royce climbed smoothly, looking well ahead to pick the best route, constantly adjusting his body for holds before he reached them so that when they came his hands and feet were in the right places. Twice he paused, to consider how to attack the next bit, but each time the delay was only momentary. He had no trouble with the rope – Brogan was paying it out without tug or jerk. Thirty feet up, there was a ledge sufficiently large to provide a good stance. Royce anchored to a knob of rock, took in the slack, and passed the rope behind him. 'On belay,' he called down. He preferred the precise expression to the casual 'Right' or 'Okay' – there was less risk of a misunderstanding.

Brogan called 'Climbing!' and began to ascend. Once more, Royce watched him carefully – and once more, with satisfaction. Brogan had said he was good on rock – and he was. He climbed with the weight on his feet, using his hands mainly for balance and not to haul himself up. His body was held well away from the rock, allowing him a good view of the holds; his hands were kept low so that the blood could feed the muscles. His progress was rhythmic, his movements confident. There was no shuffling of feet, no changing of mind. He climbed in silence, concentrating on the job. He was using exactly the same holds as Royce had used, which meant he'd kept a close eye on his leader. As he reached the stance and took over the anchor, Royce decided he need have no further anxiety about his companion's skill. Technically, Brogan was in the top rank. It was a huge relief.

The morning's climb was as challenging as Royce had expected. Some of the pitches called for no more than the varied techniques of the expert rock climber – the hold of hand or fist jammed in a crack, the friction hold, the underhold, the 'press-and-push', the knee jam, the rope threaded behind a chockstone or the knot wedged in a rock slit. Others were practicable only after artificial holds had been provided by pitons hammered into cracks. That, too, was normal routine on such a mountain. A greater problem was the lack of good stances, requiring very often a run-out of the rope so long that even when it was supported intermediately by pitons and rings the running belays offered no sure safeguard. Risks were being taken, Royce knew, which on a climb for pleasure he wouldn't have considered defensible.

Even so, progress was slow, with constant

hold-ups. Some of the delays were of a kind that couldn't be avoided in any hard ascent. Patches of slippery ice had to be cleared from ledges. The selection and fixing of the right-shaped piton for a crack took time. Prising it out afterwards, so that it could be used again, often took longer. On many of the toughest pitches both men found it safer, as well as less tiring, to climb without their cumbersome rucksacks, which had to be after-hoisted on a spare rope. But the greatest time-absorber of all was the unexplored character of the face. Lacking all knowledge of what lay above him, Royce could only move by trial and error. There were pitches so severe that he would stand poised for many minutes on a set of holds, trying to work out a route that would 'go.' Sometimes he managed to get over his problem by an exceptional measure – like the use of *étriers*, short rope ladders attached to a piton – or by briefly changing places with Brogan, whose longer reach might find a salvation hold round a projecting rock. Sometimes he would make half a dozen attempts to find a way, switching direction, advancing a little farther each time – and still in the end have to give up and retrace his steps. Once, after being turned by a pitch that only expansion bolts in drilled holes would have mastered, the climbers had to descend more than fifty feet of hard-won rock for a completely fresh start. Royce took the reverse philosophically, but Brogan began to show signs of impatience. They were not doing as well as he'd hoped, and they had a long way to go.

On one slab that looked impossible, Royce resorted to a method that he'd tried only rarely. The rock was smooth below him and smooth above, except for a single small crack. To the right he could see good holds, and a way through to what looked like a promising chimney. But the holds were eighteen inches beyond his reach. He called out to Brogan, anchored fifteen feet below him, 'Are you game for a pendulum, Captain?' Brogan shouted 'Sure!' He was game for anything that would hurry the pace. Royce, well balanced on two sound footholds, stretched up and hammered a piton home into the solitary crack. He tried his weight on it and it held firm. He ran a loop of the doubled climbing rope through a snap ring, attached the ring to the piton, and made the loop fast at his waist. He looked down to satisfy himself that Brogan was secure and ready. Then he drew back as far and as high as the loop would allow and let himself go, out over space. The pendulum swing was short – but sufficient. He grabbed the handhold he'd marked down, an incut pocket; steadied himself, found a ledge with his right foot, and untied the loop. Ten feet on, he was able to anchor. Brogan climbed up to the piton, tied on his loop, and swung across the gap with the utmost nonchalance. He joined Royce on the new stance with a grin of pleasure. 'Nice work, maestro! That's saved us something.'

Royce nodded. 'It's lost us a piton and ring, though. Let's hope we've brought enough.'

The chimney proved to be the best break they had had yet. It rose almost vertically for a hundred feet, a straight wide rift in the face of the mountain with conveniently rugged sides. They took off their sacks, and Brogan made his spare rope fast to the straps and the other end of it to his waist. Then, untrammelled, they started the transit of the chimney. Though its negotiation required a good deal of effort, it presented neither hazards nor difficulties. After the exposure of the face, both men welcomed its protection as a pleasant relief from mental strain. Its width near the opening was just right for bridging and they moved up together, arms and legs astraddle, Brogan adjusting his pace to Royce's. Towards the top the chimney narrowed a little, and for the last twenty feet they had to go into a more arduous routine, with knees exerting pressure against one wall and backs against the other. They emerged on to the open face breathing hard, and hauled up their sacks.

It was now eleven o'clock, and they had been at full stretch on the mountain for over four hours with only a few sweets and the odd stick of gum for sustenance. At the top of the chimney there was a snowy ledge, large enough to give them safe sitting room on their sacks without anchoring, and they decided to call a halt there for lunch. The stop would be brief, so they didn't unrope. Brogan took off his mitts and pushed his hands up into his armpits to warm them. Royce opened up one of the ration packets and spread out the contents.

'Well, that was a pretty punishing morning,' Brogan said. 'Would have been worse, though, if it hadn't been for your pendulum. Real sneaky, that was...' He glanced down. 'How far do you reckon we've climbed, Chief?'

Royce smiled. 'Altitude, or total mileage?'

'Just height in feet, bud. I'm not interested in the length of the trail.'

Royce looked over the side of the ledge. He could see quite clearly the gully where the helicopter had landed, and the marks where its skids had settled, and their own tracks up the snow slope. 'Five hundred feet,' he said. 'Perhaps six hundred.'

Brogan grunted. 'That's about my guess... We'll be lucky to reach the half-way mark by dusk.'

'Very lucky,' Royce said. 'Still, you never know on a mountain.'

They munched in silence for a while. They

were both eating frugally – biscuits and cheese, jam, a little chocolate. Brogan was the first to finish. He took a couple of mouthfuls from his water bottle, drew on his mitts, and got up. 'Well, I'm ready when you are, Chief. I guess there's no point in hanging about here.'

Royce nodded. He had known better picnic spots. The ledge was too cramped for any leg-stretching. A light but chilly wind was blowing ice crystals down on them from above. The sky was grey and the view sombre. On the white plain at their feet, nothing moved. For all the signs of life there were, it could have been some place in Antarctica.

The second half of the day proved to be even more exacting than the first. Stances were dangerously far apart, and several times Royce had to rely on a series of running belays whose support was little more than moral. There seemed to be more glazed rock at the level they'd reached, and every pitch required the utmost caution. There were also more steep slopes of hard ice, to be crossed at risk or circuitously avoided. The best route up was as much a matter of guesswork as ever, and the hold-ups and retreats were just as frequent.

It was around three o'clock, after another brief stop for food, that the climbers ran into their first spot of serious trouble. They had

75

been going for half an hour, with fewer checks than usual, when they were faced with a traverse over rock of dubious soundness. Royce paused, weighing the risks against the possible rewards. Below the rock there was a short forty-five degree slope of frozen snow, and then the void. Unattractive – but better, at least, than a sheer drop from the face. The traverse itself was only about ten feet long. The alternative was another time-wasting retreat. Brogan, he saw, was on a good stance with a sound belay. He was correctly placed below his anchor, the loop between waist and anchor short so that he wouldn't be dragged off, his outside leg firmly planted in line with the likely pull of the doubled rope – and no unnecessary slack...

'I think I'll try it,' Royce said.

He stepped out cautiously, testing each rock projection before putting any weight on it, using his skill and experience to take full advantage of each hold. Where a foot-hold threatened to break outwards he trod flat; where a handhold was no more than a thin vertical flake he pulled downwards. Even bad rock was usually firm in some direction. Still he was far from happy. A handhold moved under his fingers. He tried another. That was loose, too. He recalled a classic phrase – 'like trying to climb library shelves by holding on to the books.' He called quietly to Brogan, 'It won't go, I'm coming back.' With infinite care, he reached for a handhold he had just left. With equal care, he transferred a little of his weight from his right foot. Then all the holds seemed to crumble at once. He was falling, and there was nothing he could do about it.

A pull at his waist checked his slide, and a sharp jerk stopped him. He looked up the slope, unhurt but shaken. He had gone down only about twelve feet, but 'coming off' was always a shock. He grasped the rope and hauled himself up to Brogan's stance. 'You okay?' Brogan asked anxiously. Royce brushed the snow from his windsmock and adjusted his balaclava, which he'd nearly lost. 'Yes, thank you,' he said. 'Your sliding arrest was text-book.' He grinned. 'In future, I think I'll call you "Colonel"!'

It took them some time to find an alternative route. The pitch they finally managed was very severe, with a long slab that ended in an overhang and involved much hammering in of pitons and a great expenditure of energy. The effort, however, brought an unexpected reward. At the top they came out on a broad, deep ledge that sloped slightly inwards from the face. Royce took one look at it, and made up his mind. 'We'll camp here,' he said.

Brogan's face registered dismay. 'Hell, Chief, we've still got a good hour of daylight ahead.'

'I know – but where will we be in an hour, if we go on?'

'Higher up,' Brogan said. 'That's for sure.'

'Yes – and perhaps clinging to a piton all night. You know the rule – always give away a bit of height for the sake of a good bivouac. On any other mountain, you'd agree at once.'

'Maybe – but this isn't any other mountain. We've got to make that summit by tomorrow.'

'We shan't do it by tiring ourselves out,' Royce said.

For a moment, Brogan looked as though he was going to go on arguing. Then he shrugged, and took off his sack. 'Okay, have it your own way. You're the boss.'

6

They took off their crampons, unroped, and put on extra sweaters to maintain their climbing warmth as long as possible. Brogan inspected the nylon rope to make sure there were no cuts and, when he was satisfied, coiled it expertly. He seemed to have recovered from his sharp annoyance over the early bivouac, but was still a little quiet and thoughtful. While he worked on the rope Royce cleared an area of snow with his ice-axe and erected the two-man tent, a simple A-type with a sewn-in groundsheet and a sleeve entrance. He used pitons in cracks to hold the fore-and-aft guys, aluminium pegs around the foot, and snow to anchor the sides. The wind had dropped, and with the temperature only just below freezing they could look forward to a reasonably snug night.

While Brogan filled the melting-pot with ice chips from the ledge, Royce got out the aluminium hot-water bottle that contained the petrol and started up the stove. By the time the ration of dried food was well soaked and they were ready to begin cooking, it was almost dark. Royce lit a candle and stuck it in a matchbox. By its dim light he boiled oatmeal, added meat bar, vegetable and egg, with a little extra salt to make up the day's loss, and stirred the mixture into a thick 'hoosh' which he divided carefully between the two billycans.

They ate with relish and sharp appetite. 'I guess we'll find this stuff pretty nauseating before we're through,' Brogan said, as he scraped out his last fragment with a plastic spoon, 'but it sure tastes good to-night.' Afterwards they made coffee, using the day's ration of dried milk and sugar, and finished off with chocolate and sweets.

As soon as the meal was over they spread all their spare clothes on the groundsheet to give some insulation from the icy rock and got into their down sleeping sacks. Brogan stretched out with a cigarette. Royce lit his pipe. He liked a pipe after a climbing day – it went well with the peace and silence and encouraged tranquil reflection. He felt replete in body and contented in mind. Camping in the mountains could be as great a pleasure as climbing them, when conditions were good. Not that there was anything to get lyrical about on this ledge. There were no lavender evening shadows, no intriguing outlines of rock against a luminous sky, no waving grasses, no gentle breezes on the face, no stars. Nothing poetical or romantic or symbolic. Just raw cold – accompanied, unless Royce's ears deceived him, by the high-pitched howl of wolves in the plain below... All the same, he could think of nowhere he would sooner be.

Royce's love of mountains was a comprehensive passion. Climbing to him was an aesthetic pleasure, a health-giving outlet for his physical energy, a science and a craft whose developed skills gave him a deep and abiding satisfaction. A craft with a limitless variety of demands on strength and will, endurance and nerve; a craft where no two situations were ever quite the same, where each new challenge had to be met by a fresh call on ingenuity and resource. A craft that produced a wealth of memories and experiences and friendships, to enjoy in the present and store for the future.

Climbing gave him the excitement of achievement – the thrill of pitting himself against the forces of nature, of possessing the hills. It tested his abilities as an organiser; it gave him the satisfaction of good leadership unobtrusively exercised; of thinking for a whole roped party, of binding it by the strength of his personality, by tact and firmness and example, into an effective team.

And that wasn't all. The high mountains, to Royce, were a place of dignity and freedom – remote from urban squalor, safe from the builder and developer, free from the scourge of motor cars, avoided by aircraft – clean and wholesome and eternally wrapped in silence. A sanctuary and a haven. The last redoubt against the march of progress...

He lay with his head on his rucksack, thinking over the day's events. It had been a good climb, full of technical interest and not too exhausting. They had taken some chances – but chances had been implicit in the nature of the operation. The 'library shelves' had been a calculated risk, and Royce's fall an incident of no consequence. At the pace they were climbing, and on very severe rock, minor slips were bound to occur. Coming off was always disagreeable, but nothing worse – as long as the belaying was good and the fall a short one, quickly arrested...

He thought about Brogan, his excellent

companion. He couldn't have wished for a better backer-up. A fine practitioner, Brogan – a real mountain craftsman. A man who could be completely relied on in any tight spot. Very different in temperament, of course, from Royce himself. Less highly strung, less imaginative. Royce knew himself well. Self-mastery in the mountains had not come easily to him. He had had to learn to discipline his judgment, learn to keep a cool head, learn to control his nerves. Brogan, on the other hand, appeared to have no nerves. He had taken that quite sensational pendulum swing as though it had been a step across a stream. He seemed to be one of those rare men who didn't know what fear was. A great quality, and in some situations a great asset – though it had its dangers. It could lead to impetuosity – and Brogan *was* a little impetuous. At least on this climb, where the objective obviously meant so much more to him than the climb itself…

Brogan suddenly spoke – and it was almost as though he'd been reading Royce's thoughts. 'Tell me, Chief – just why did you decide to come on this trip?'

Royce puffed quietly at his pipe for a moment. Then he said, 'For the adventure, I suppose, it was irresistible.'

'Just that – the challenge of the mountain? Breaking new ground? Getting some place no one had ever been before?'

82

'Well, the idea of beating the Russians to the top was quite attractive. I enjoy a race as much as anyone.'

Brogan grunted. 'I didn't get the impression you were in that much of a hurry to-day.'

'Oh, come off it!' Royce said. 'I want us to get to the top in one piece, that's all.'

'You're not too bothered about the camera, though, are you? You don't really care what happens to it?'

'I'm probably not as concerned about it as you are,' Royce said.

'Why not?'

'Well, for one thing, I imagine the Russians will soon get the secret anyway. They've got so many agents, they always manage to, somehow. I'm sure it's only a matter of time.'

'Time can be pretty important,' Brogan said. 'Ever tried holding a hand grenade with the pin out?'

Royce smiled. 'You've got a point there.'

'After all, you heard what the general said. Lives could be saved by an invention like this. American lives. Even British lives. Maybe the Commies will get to know all about it in the end – but so what? The thing that matters is always to have the edge on them.'

'That's the short-term view, yes.'

'What other view is there, unless you're on their side?'

'There's the long-term view,' Royce said.

'How do you mean? I don't get you.'

'Well, all these great idealogical conflicts pass – like the old religious wars. They're forgotten, and others take their place. All the struggles seem terribly important at the time – but in the long run what do they achieve?'

'Progress, maybe.'

'I'd say change, rather than progress. A different arrangement of the pieces... Take this country we're in now – Turkey. Not so long ago the Ottoman Empire consisted of Asia Minor, parts of Russia, the Ukraine, the Crimea, the Balkans, most of north Africa and the whole of Arabia. Generations of men fought and died to build it up. Hundreds of thousands of innocents were massacred to extend it. And now look at it. What was it all for?'

Brogan shrugged. 'I guess it's just human nature to struggle.'

'I agree – but it doesn't make human nature very sensible. If every generation insists on fighting someone, and no good comes of it, on a long view it seems pretty stupid to take sides.'

'Well, that's not the way I see it,' Brogan said. 'It's all very well being that high-and-mighty, but you can't stand back from life. I've seen these Commie guys at close quarters and I don't like them. I don't like what they do to people. Would you want to be taken over by them?'

'Certainly not.'

'Would you fight to prevent it?'

'I expect so, if it was the only way... I'm human, too.'

'Then on the short view we're on the same side?'

'That's right,' Royce said.

'And you've no short-term objection to me blowing up that camera?'

'None at all. If I had I wouldn't be here.'

'Then what the hell are we arguing about?'

Royce grinned. 'I don't know, Captain. You started it!'

7

Both men were awake and on the move well before dawn next day, completely refreshed after a good night's sleep and eager to tackle the remaining sixteen hundred feet or so of the mountain. They breakfasted by candlelight, on sweet tea, biscuits and jam, and by first light were packed, cramponed, roped up and ready to leave. There had been no appreciable change in the weather during the night except that the cloud base had lifted a little, unveiling features which they hadn't previously been aware of. The most disconcerting was a near-perpendicular wall of black rock just below cloud level, extending like a fringe to east and west across the mountain as far as the eye could see. Day

Two was evidently going to present even tougher problems than Day One.

Royce led off slowly as usual, getting his eye in, getting used again to the feel of the rock under his fingers and of his crampons on the icy ledges. But as soon as they were moving well, he quickened his pace – and he also made a time-saving change in the climbing arrangements. From now on, he said, they would 'climb through,' taking the lead alternately – a mark of confidence which Brogan appreciated, and which avoided the necessity of handing over the anchor at each stance.

There was one brief interruption in the first hour, when the sound of an engine broke the silence. 'The chopper!' Brogan called, pointing outwards at the growing speck. The helicopter flew parallel to the face for a few minutes, obviously looking for them. Then the pilot spotted them, and hovered and waved, before flying off. It was no more than a routine check, but both men welcomed it as a sign that the promised eye was being kept on them. Apart from the helicopter – and, once, a solitary eagle that planed away on ragged wings – the mountain and the ground below were as still and lifeless as ever.

The climbers made excellent progress to the foot of the black rock wall. There, on a safe anchorage, they halted, and dismally surveyed its precipitous face. No long inspection was needed to tell them that with the equipment they carried it was unscalable at the point they'd reached. The possible holds were far apart, there were no cracks for pitons, and there was no sign of an adequate stance within the limits of their rope.

They looked to east and west. From where they stood, the bastion seemed to offer equally poor prospects in both directions. Royce tossed a coin, and they began a traverse to the left, hoping for a change in the character of the rocks that would allow them to resume the ascent. The going was slow and hazardous, with more reliance on running belays than either of them liked, and almost total exposure below. By mid-morning they had advanced horizontally for several hundred feet without finding any break in the smooth slab above them. Then even the traverse became impossible. They were turned by a vertical outcrop that they couldn't climb over or round, and they had no choice but to retrace their steps.

They paused for food and a brief rest at the stance where they'd tossed the coin, and then started to traverse in the opposite direction. This time they were luckier. After an hour's hard going, the outlook suddenly improved. The peculiarly smooth rock formation above them, though still unclimbable, was tapering to the east. By midday they could see its end. What was more, there was an open field of snow beyond it, rising into the cloud at a steady forty-five degrees. It looked like a quick way to the summit and their hopes rose – only to be dashed again at once. Before they could reach it, a new and formidable obstacle held them up – an ice slope below the wall, some fifty feet across. It extended outwards for about thirty feet at an angle of at least sixty degrees, ending in a sheer drop of more than two thousand feet to the plain.

Royce prodded the ice cautiously with the point of his axe. He had rarely seen a surface he less liked the look of. It was glassy and flaky, the kind that could disintegrate at a blow. To attempt to cut steps or drive in pitons was unthinkable. To try and cross its fifty feet with no other support than the initial anchorage would be to invite a slide over the precipice, a long free fall and a broken rope.

He examined the rock above the slope. It appeared to offer neither holds nor cracks. It was an unbroken slab all the way, for as high as a hand could reach.

The two men looked at each other. Brogan's face was stiff with disappointment. The very nearness of success made the situation all the more galling. If they could cross that sloping sheet of ice, they'd be as good as on the summit. If they couldn't, there was no way open to them to the top – and the expedition would have failed.

Brogan said gloomily, 'Got anything to suggest, Chief?'

Royce gazed at the slope and shook his head. 'If we can't get support from the rock, I'm afraid we've had it.'

'Would the glasses help?'

Royce got out his binoculars and focused them on the rock wall above the ice, ranging along its whole length. He lingered for a moment on a point about halfway across, passed on, and returned to it. He adjusted the focus of the glasses, wiped the lenses, and made another long inspection.

'I believe I can see one small crack,' he said at last. 'It's either that or a dark line in the rock. About five feet up. Take a look.'

Brogan looked. Presently he nodded. 'Could be. It's hard to tell from here.'

'If it is a crack,' Royce said, 'and we could get a piton in, we might just make it.'

He stood quietly, weighing the risks. A fall before he reached the crack – if it was a crack – or a fall from a piton in the centre, would still keep him on the slope and not let him go over the edge. It should be manageable...

'I think it's worth a bash,' he said. He tucked his piton hammer through his waist loop, and tied piton and snap ring separately to the loop so that they'd be handy when he needed them. Then, treading as delicately as though he were walking on eggshells, he moved out on to the slope, balancing on the four frontal teeth of his crampons, hugging the shaft of his ice axe under one arm and grasping the head with both hands, pick downwards, ready to arrest his fall if he came off. Brogan paid out the rope, watching in tense silence.

It took Royce a full five minutes to reach the dark line on the wall. It *was* a crack, of the right width and in sound rock. Poised on his crampon points, scarcely daring to breathe, he groped for the piton-lashing at his waist, untied it, and inserted the piton into the crack. With the same deliberation he drew out the piton hammer and began to tap the piton. As soon as it was far enough in to have any grip at all, he fixed the snap ring to it. Now he had something to support him. Holding on to the ring, he hammered the piton home. Then he passed the climbing rope through the ring in a running belay.

He turned and gave the thumbs-up sign to Brogan. 'All right so far,' he called. He looked across the slope to a stance he had marked down just beyond the ice. It was slightly below his level – a shallow, snow-covered ledge, with a needle of rock above it that would make a good anchor if he ever got there. He started off again, on a slanting traverse, moving with cat-like steps. He was barely a yard from his objective when there was an ominous crack. A moment later the ice crumpled under his crampons. His feet shot from under him and he slithered down, gathering momentum, trying to check his fall with the pick of his axe. There was a hellish jerk at his waist that almost drove the breath from his body – and the motion stopped. He was lying on his stomach on the slope. He looked up. Everything had held – Brogan, the piton and the rope. He was only five feet above the edge of the precipice – but safe.

He called out to Brogan that he was all right. For a few seconds he lay quietly on the slope, recovering his wind. Then he hauled himself back to the piton, got to his feet, and stood balanced there, grasping the ring and surveying the scene.

The ice slope had shattered. Between him and his needle of rock, some twenty-five feet away, there was nothing now but a mass of unstable ice fragments that would give no grip at all. There wasn't a hope he could make it.

Not, at least, by orthodox methods… He looked across at the needle, measuring the distance with his eye, sizing up the difficulty. It would be a long shot – so long that ordinarily he wouldn't have considered it. But in their present situation it was worth a try…

He called again to Brogan. 'Make a noose in your spare rope – about four feet in diameter. Try to throw it to me.' While he waited, he tied himself to the snap ring with a doubled rope sling, so that both his hands were left free.

It took Brogan only a few moments to make the noose and coil the rope for a throw. His first cast fell a foot short and the rope slid away down the slope. His second was accurate. A loop struck Royce's arm and he grabbed it. He hauled in thirty feet of slack, coiled it carefully, leaned away from the rock on his sling, and aimed the noose at the needle.

He cast twelve times without success, hauling the rope back each time and re-coiling the slack. At the thirteenth throw the noose caught on the top of the needle. Royce gave the rope a shake and the noose slid down to the bottom.

The rest was easy. Brogan pulled the rope-bar taut and made it fast at his stance. Royce worked his way along it to the needle and anchored there.

Brogan shouted, 'Do you want to take the spare, or shall we leave it fixed?'

Royce considered. Without a fixed rope, it would be impossible for them to return that way. But he doubted whether they could afford to abandon one of their spares at this stage, not knowing what problems lay ahead. Better to take a chance on finding a different route for the descent. He cupped his hands and called across the gap, 'We'll take it.'

Brogan waved in acknowledgment, and released the spare, and re-tied it through a snap ring with a cunning knot. Then he made a quick, safe passage, carrying the free end with him. When he reached the new stance he gave a sharp jerk on the end of the rope, the distant knot undid itself, and he hauled in.

He turned to Royce gripping his hand. 'Gee, that was a swell job, Chief. Sure you're not damaged?'

'A bit bruised,' Royce said. 'Nothing serious.' He wiped a trace of blood from a graze on his chin, and grinned. 'You know, Captain – when you get back you'll be able to say something that no one has ever been able to say before.'

'What's that?'

'"I went climbing with Bill Royce and he came off twice in twenty-four hours!"'

Brogan laughed. 'Not me! And there's something else I won't ever tell anyone.'

'Oh? – what?'

'That I was raised on a ranch in Wyoming – and it was you who thought of the lasso!'

8

They rested at the stance for a few minutes, munching chocolate, quenching their thirst from bottles they'd replenished with melted snow at the overnight bivouac, and discussing with grim pleasure the obstacle they'd overcome and the details of the transit. Then, in the best of spirits, they set off on what they hoped would be the last stage of the ascent.

This time their hopes were realised. A couple of easy pitches took them clear of the rock face and on to the snow field, and from there the climb was straightforward. The surface was of old, hard snow, melted and re-frozen, and not in any danger of sliding. They cramponed straight up, gaining height rapidly. In a few minutes they had penetrated the cloud base. Royce headed in a north-westerly direction, aiming for the true summit rather than the ridge where the plane had crashed – and Brogan didn't object. After the long, gruelling struggle, they both felt they had to stand on the top before they did anything else.

The cloud was thinner than it had seemed from below, and patchier. It swirled around them, sometimes closing in until they could barely see each other, sometimes parting to reveal quite long vistas of snow ahead. Occasionally, a gap would open, giving them a bird's eye view of the plain three thousand feet below. Most of the time, visibility was about thirty yards. With the cloud near freezing point, and a noticeable wind, conditions were no longer even moderately pleasant. Hoar frost settled on the climbers' balaclavas, and whitened their eyebrows and their two days' growth of beard. Breathing, in the cold thin air, was difficult. Purely from the weather point of view, Royce could scarcely remember a climb that had been so uniformly raw and uninspiring. Still, like Brogan, he was warmed and heartened by the nearness of the summit.

They came to the top in a most undramatic way, plodding on uphill till there was no more uphill to climb. The summit was quite unspectacular – a flattened cone of softer, deeper snow, without a single visible feature. But as they made an exploratory circuit of the cone, its very lack of feature was a source of satisfaction. There were no human tracks, no marks of any kind. The snow was virgin. If they *had* been engaged in a race with the Russians, they had won it.

Royce got out his large-scale map. Brogan held one corner, steadying it against the wind, and they studied it together, refreshing their memory of direction and distance. The ridge where the crashed plane had been sighted was shown as running slightly north of east for about two hundred yards from where they stood, and then curving sharply to the north for another hundred yards to the point marked on the map with a red X. Royce established the direction with his compass and drew an arrow in the snow.

'That should lead us to the wreck,' he said. 'What do you want to do, Captain – search for it right away? We've still got a bit of daylight.'

Brogan nodded. 'I figure it's too late to do anything about the camera to-night, but we could find some place to camp close by. Then we'll be all set for the morning.'

'I agree.' Royce took a few steps in the direction the arrow was pointing, studying the ground, looking ahead as far as the cloud would let him. The surface of the snow was smooth and regular, unmarked by any hollows or breaks that might mean hidden crevasses. 'Let's unrope,' he said, 'we'll be more comfortable. Even a couple of hundred yards in this stuff are going to be quite a drag.'

They dumped their sacks, freed themselves from their restricting waist loops, coiled the climbing rope, took off and wrapped their crampons, and re-packed. Royce was about to shoulder his sack and move off when he suddenly gave a sharp exclamation and pointed. 'Look...!'

A large gap had opened in the bank of cloud to the east, exposing the lower part of the ridge – the part where it curved to the north. At its edge, a dark, slim shape was emerging against the background of snow. The fuselage of a plane...

Royce got out his glasses and focused them on the wreck. The fuselage looked more battered at close range than the aerial picture had suggested, but it was clearly still in one piece. A long, broad track showed where it had skidded over the snow before coming to rest. Bits of wreckage were scattered all around it – an engine, a piece of wing with the R.A.F.'s red, white and blue roundel on it, a litter of shapeless debris. If there were bodies, they were not distinguishable.

Royce concentrated again on the fuselage. A wisp of cloud had moved away, and now he could see its position on the ridge more plainly. What he saw was startling. He passed the glasses to Brogan. 'Our troubles are only just beginning,' he said. 'Take a look.'

Brogan looked. 'Oh, jeeze!' he exclaimed. The fuselage was lying near the tip of one of the largest snow overhangs he had ever seen – some sixty feet of bulging, stratified protuberance, stretching out unsupported over what appeared to be a very deep *couloir*. And that wasn't all. Across the south-facing back of the cornice there was a dark depression that clearly showed a line of weakness... Brogan was still gazing at it when the cloud closed in and the view was blotted out.

He passed the glasses back to Royce. 'You're right, Chief. That sure is going to be a problem.'

'Well, at least we know what's there,' Royce said. 'We were lucky. If the gap hadn't opened when it did, we might easily have blundered on to the overhang without realising the danger... Right, let's find a place to camp.'

The few hundred yards down the ridge proved a trying slog at the end of a hard day. The snow was deep, with a crust too thin to bear their weight, so that at every step they sank to their thighs and sometimes to their waists. Repeatedly they had to stop and remove with their axes the huge balls of snow that collected under their boots and made every movement as ponderous as a diver's. Their route, under the lee of the south flank, was as sheltered as any they could find, but even there the wind was biting. When they finally reached a point they judged to be roughly opposite the wreck, both men were thankful to call a halt. The long traverse under the bastion and the tense moments on the ice slope, culminating in this wade along the summit ridge, had tired them out.

They found a flattish surface on the southern slope, stamped out a platform in the snow, and quickly pitched their tent in the failing light, using pitons to secure the guy ropes and piling blocks of snow on the sod-cloth to keep the edges down. Once inside, with their boots off and their socks wrung out and the petrol stove hotting up the 'hoosh' and the atmosphere, their tiredness fell away. Royce, in particular, was soon basking in the pleasant glow of achievement. Even by his high standards, the two-day climb had been a great one. They had attacked an unknown mountain of extreme severity in poor conditions, fought their way over the worst it could offer, and reached the summit triumphantly on schedule. For the moment, that was enough for him.

Brogan's frame of mind was different. He was subdued and thoughtful through the meal, obviously dwelling on the task ahead. As Royce handed him his beaker of coffee, he started to talk about it. 'You had much experience of cornices, Chief?'

'Quite a bit,' Royce said.

'Mine's pretty limited ... I know a heck of a lot of good men have lost their lives on them.'

Royce nodded. 'Often on the very big ones. They're the ones that look solid – so you don't suspect them until it's too late.'

'They usually break without any warning – isn't that right?'

'Yes – and much higher up than you'd imagine. The only safe way is to give them a very wide berth.'

'Have you got any views about this one?'

'Not till I've had a closer look at it,' Royce said.

'If it stood the weight of the fuselage crashing down and sliding over it, it should be able to stand the weight of a man.'

'There's always the last straw.'

'Yeah... Well, I guess we'll just have to

figure out a way of anchoring that'll lessen the risk. Maybe if we drove in the ice axes a good way apart, well down the back of the cornice and sort of flanking it, the nylon would hold me in the middle without too much of a fall if the overhang collapsed.'

'The snow's very soft,' Royce said. 'A fall could easily pull out the axes.'

'Maybe... But can you suggest anything better?'

Royce puffed thoughtfully at his pipe. 'If we could find a good crack in the rock on each side of the cornice, near its root, we might be able to drive in pitons and stretch a rope taut over the top. That would give us a safe anchor. But you could still have a hell of a fall – and how would you get up again? You'd be swinging free – I couldn't pull you up on my own.'

'I could fit myself out with a couple of those Prusik slings you've brought, and haul myself up – like out of a crevasse.'

'Have you ever tried to do that?'

'Nope. Never had to. But I know the theory.'

'It isn't at all easy the first time – especially if the rope happens to be wet. I'd say it was a pretty desperate measure.'

'We're up against a desperate situation,' Brogan said. 'I've got to get out on that overhang somehow or I won't be able to do the job... And I haven't climbed three thousand feet of rock to be beaten by a bloody cornice.'

Royce grunted. 'Well, we'll take a good look at it in the morning. Let's hope the cloud thins a bit.'

'Yeah… What's it like now?'

Royce thrust his hands into the sleeve opening of the tent, pulled its sides apart, and stuck his head out. He drew back quickly, brushing white flakes from his face. 'It looks as though the weather may settle the problem for us,' he said. 'At the moment, it's snowing hard.'

9

Royce had a rather disturbed night, which he put down to aching muscles and bruises from his second fall. He was already awake when the first light of day penetrated the fabric of the tent. It was a very dim light, hardly distinguishable from dusk, and it seemed to grow no stronger as time went by. When he put his head through the sleeve opening and looked out, he saw why. Nearly six inches of fresh snow had fallen during the night, covering the tent in an opaque blanket. The snow was still coming down, not heavily, but in large, wet flakes. Evidently the temperature had risen. The enveloping cloud was denser, and visibility was down to a few yards. It was a grey and murky scene, wholly uninviting.

Brogan stirred and raised his head. 'What's it like, Chief?'

'Filthy!' Royce told him.

'Any chance of a move?'

'Not the slightest,' Royce said. 'I'm going to turn in again.'

They breakfasted around ten, taking their time over the meal and the few chores that followed. Afterwards they put on their boots and wind smocks and made a tentative sortie. Once they were away from the shelter of the south flank, conditions were even worse than they'd imagined. A strong wind was blowing from the north-west, driving the snow before it almost horizontally. The air was thick with it – a near white-out. Walking was more difficult than ever. Even Brogan agreed that there was no point in going to look at the cornice till the weather improved. There'd be little to see and nothing they could do. All they'd achieve would be a loss of body temperature in the raw cold.

They spent an unusually silent morning in the tent. Royce would have been happy to chat, to pass the time in climbing reminiscences, to exchange views on this and that. But Brogan was taciturn, talking only when a remark was addressed to him and quickly drying up. It was obvious that he was chafing for action and could think of nothing but the job ahead. He got out his wire and battery and detonators and checked them over. He got out his gun and cleaned it. He got out one of the Prusik slings and examined it, and practised tying the special Prusik knot. He smoked a lot of cigarettes. Royce, respecting his mood, was content to lie and doze. When the weather was bad, he believed in conserving energy.

Some time after lunch, the light improved. Brogan went out on another reconnaissance and returned quickly to report that the wind was dropping and the snow dying out. 'I reckon we could get cracking now, Chief. I've been out on mountains in plenty worse conditions than this. I've climbed in worse.'

Royce turned a sock that he'd hung up to dry on an improvised line. 'So have I,' he said. 'But not around cornices. Particularly after a heavy snow fall and a rise in temperature. That's just when they break.'

'We could try driving in those pitons you were talking about, and maybe get the rope across. We wouldn't need to go out on the overhang for that.'

Royce shook his head. 'I don't think so, Captain. The whole place could be unstable with all this new snow around on top of the old. I should hang on for a bit. By to-morrow, everything may be frozen hard again.'

'Suppose it isn't?'

'Well,' Royce said, 'we'll still have a little time.'

'How much time? When's the deadline for leaving?'

Royce considered. 'I'd say the day after to-morrow, around noon.'

'As late as that?'

'I think so. It's running it a bit fine, per-haps, but I'd be prepared to stay till then if necessary.'

'We've got to find a new route, don't forget.'

'I know,' Royce said, 'but we'll probably be able to rope down a good part of the way. With ordinary luck, the descent should be much quicker than the climb up.'

'Would the food hold out that long?'

'Just about. We'd have a last ration for the evening bivouac on the day we left – after that we'd have to make a dash for it. But I think we'd manage. And on that basis, you've got nearly forty-eight hours to tackle the cornice. So my advice, Captain, is to wait.'

Brogan gave a reluctant nod. 'Yeah – I guess that all figures... Okay, Chief – I'll hang on and see what to-morrow brings.'

The afternoon dragged slowly by. There was no more snow, but the cloud showed no sign of lifting. By four o'clock it was already beginning to get dark. Brogan had rolled back the tent sleeve to let in more air and was sitting by the gap, gloomily gazing out at nothing. Royce was feeling in his rucksack for a fresh candle.

Suddenly Brogan leaned forward, his ear to the opening. 'Listen?' he said.

Royce joined him. 'What is it?'

'I thought I heard voices.'

Royce crouched down beside him. They listened, tensely. For a moment, all was silence. Then an unmistakable sound reached them. A man's voice, shouting.

Brogan sprang to life. 'It's the Russkies...!' He snatched up his gun and rammed it in the pocket of his wind smock. 'Come on, let's go see what's happening.'

Royce pulled on his boots, eyeing the butt of the gun. 'I hope you're not thinking of shooting anyone, Captain. There were to be no incidents – remember?'

'Don't worry – I won't shoot unless someone shoots at me.' Brogan climbed out through the sleeve. Royce followed him. Together they ploughed their way up the flank of the ridge in the direction of the voices. They could hear two men talking now. As they reached the top Brogan grabbed Royce and pulled him down into the snow. 'There they are! – right ahead.'

Royce peered through the gathering gloom. Two men, roped together, had just climbed up over the lip of the *couloir*, fifty yards to the west of the wrecked plane. Two short men, bulky with padded clothes and huge rucksacks and big fur hats with earflaps tied above. One of them had thrust his ice axe into the snow as an anchor and was taking in slack. Presently a third man came over the edge, just as bulky and shapeless, and joined them. The three stood together, talking, laughing, shaking hands. There was a short consultation, and they began to unrope.

Royce said softly, 'They must be damn' good climbers to have got up that *couloir* in cloud and a snow storm. Or else very lucky.'

Brogan grunted. 'To hell with their climbing! They're on Turkish soil – and they shouldn't be.'

Royce looked at him wryly. 'What are you going to do about it, Captain? Ask to see their visas?'

'That depends on what they do next,' Brogan said – and took out his gun.

The Russians had finished their conference. After a moment they began to move off eastwards along the ridge, plodding in single file through the deep snow. They sounded very cheerful, and very purposeful. Presently one of them stopped and pointed over to the left and they changed direction. Now they were heading straight for the plane wreck.

Brogan got to his feet. 'Just what I thought!' he said. '*They're* not going to worry about the cornice – and they're not even roped. Goddamit, why did I sit on my ass all day?' He set off again up the slope, keeping the Russians just in sight through the cloud and the falling dusk. Royce ploughed along silently beside him.

They stopped just short of the overhang, gazing ahead. One of the Russians was only a few yards in front of them, fixing a boot. The other two were out on the cornice. They had dumped their sacks beside the fuselage and were walking around it. One of them began to sing. The other laughed, and joined in noisily. Then, unbelievably, he went into a dance routine, down on his haunches.

Royce gripped Brogan's arm. 'For God's sake – they can't know...! They can't possibly know.' For a moment he stood watching them in silent horror. Then he plunged forward, shouting the only warning he thought might be understood. 'Stop! *Stop!*'

He was too late. Almost without a sound, the cornice collapsed. The singer, the dancer, the fuselage and the great block of snow and ice simply disappeared. There was a faint cry, then silence. Seconds later, a low rumble came up from the depths. After that, the silence was unbroken.

10

The three who were left stared out into the

void, frozen into immobility by the swiftness, the awful finality, of the disaster.

It was Royce who moved first. He walked past the Russian survivor and approached as near as he dared to the fractured edge. He looked down. Cloud and darkness filled the *couloir.* Nothing was visible. He stood listening. He could hear nothing.

He had no doubt that the two men were dead. They had fallen a long way before hitting the ground – at least a hundred feet, to judge by the delayed rumble of the impact. Only a miracle could have prevented them being killed instantly. In any case, no search was practicable till daylight. On a fine night, with head lamps, it might have been possible. In cloud and darkness it was out of the question.

He turned sombrely away. He had seen men die on mountains before. Several times – and some of them his friends. He was a realist about it. As long as there were climbers, rock and ice would take their toll. It was the price the mountain exacted for supreme moments. But it was always a shock, and it always saddened him – particularly when the deaths could have been avoided.

He joined Brogan. Together they approached the Russian. The man was rocking to and fro, hands crossed over his chest, murmuring strange words that sounded like *'Bozhe moi.'* As Royce and Brogan drew near, he stiffened and became silent.

He was swaddled in a quilted jacket and quilted breeches, like the two who had fallen. He was wearing the same kind of fur hat. At a distance, he looked exactly like them. But something about the timbre of his voice caused Royce to peer closer into his face. In the bad light there was little to see – but there was enough. 'Good God,' Royce said, 'it's a girl!'

Brogan stared down in disbelief – and groaned. 'That's all we needed!'

The girl suddenly spoke. 'Do not worry,' she said in English. 'I shall give you no trouble.' Her speech was precise and almost accentless.

'A linguist!' Brogan exclaimed. 'Well – surprise, surprise!'

The girl looked from one to the other. 'I was warned that I might meet Americans at the summit. Are you American?'

'*I* am,' Brogan said. 'My friend's British.'

'It is almost the same thing.'

Brogan snorted. 'You think so?'

'What is the difference? Both your countries are the enemies of mine.'

There was an awkward silence. Then Royce said gently, 'Might I suggest a private truce? Our countries may not be exactly friendly, but we've all climbed the same mountain and faced the same dangers. We've all been witnesses of the same terrible disaster. We've all got to spend the night up here. Why don't we go to the tent and try to behave in a civilised way?'

The girl hesitated.

'You'll be safe enough,' Brogan told her. 'It's not the Lubianka jail.'

Royce said, 'Easy, Captain – that's no way to start a truce!'

The girl pulled her ice axe out of the snow. 'Very well – I will come... No doubt we shall be able to talk better there.'

Royce led the way down the slope to the camp. He entered the tent first, and lit a candle. The girl dumped her axe and rucksack at the entrance and squeezed herself through the sleeve. Brogan followed her in. There was barely room for the three of them, but by arranging themselves carefully they all managed to sit.

Royce studied the girl. Below the fur hat he saw an oval face with high cheek bones, framed in jet black hair; dark eyes under dark eyebrows, superciliously arched; a full, arrogant mouth. It was a face of strength and character, self-assured and invincibly hostile. Conversation was not going to be easy.

He tried a little sympathy. 'May I say how very sorry I am about the accident? I wish it could have been avoided. I tried to warn you.'

'Not until it was too late,' the girl said.

'I assure you that wasn't intentional. At first I took it for granted you all knew what you were doing.'

The girl was silent for a moment. Then she said, 'We were careless – I admit it. We were climbing in cloud, with no clear view of the ridge, and we should have investigated. We were excited at finding the aeroplane, and forgot everything else.'

Royce nodded. 'A great tragedy for you.'

'It is always tragic when good men die on mountains. Or anywhere else.'

'Were they personal friends of yours?'

'No ... I met them once at a Congress of Alpinists, and the second time was yesterday... But when you climb with others, on one rope, they quickly become your friends.'

'That's very true.'

There was another pause. Then Brogan said, 'How come you speak English so well?'

'It is my work,' the girl said. 'I speak many languages. In Moscow I am an interpreter for the Ministry of Foreign Affairs.'

'No kidding... Did you come here from Moscow?'

'Yes. I flew to Tbilisi, where I met my two comrades. From there we were brought by helicopter to the mountain.'

'When did you start the climb?' Royce asked.

'At noon yesterday. Our schedule provided for twenty-two hours of climbing, but we improved upon it – though conditions were extremely difficult... And you?'

'We took a little longer. About twenty-four hours of climbing, from the foot.'

The girl nodded. 'You were hoping to recover the camera, of course?'

'Something like that,' Royce said.

'And you have failed.'

'Obviously we have… As a matter of interest, what were *you* planning to do about the camera?'

'We were going to remove it and lower it into the *couloir*. A helicopter was to pick it up later. Now – I do not know. I think it will be impossible.'

Brogan said, 'What did your people tell you about the aeroplane?'

'They said it was one of your planes – a spy plane that flew over the Soviet Union to photograph our secrets. That was why it was necessary for us to get the camera.'

'Yeah! Well, Miss… What is your name, by the way?'

'My family name is Lermontov.'

'Well, Miss Lermontov, just for the record – that plane was no spy plane. We don't use them these days – we use satellites. That plane was operating peacefully over Germany when it was diverted to Russia by a Soviet agent at the point of a gun. It was stolen, because it had a secret camera on board that your people wanted. *Our* secret, *our* camera. When the crew managed to get control of the plane again, and tried to fly it out, your people shot it down in cold blood. Hi-jacking and murder – that's what it was.'

The girl shrugged. 'Naturally you would say something like that. I am sorry, but I do not believe you.'

'I didn't expect you would,' Brogan said. 'But it so happens it's true. On our side of the Curtain, we don't put out false stories about these things. Apart from anything else, we know we wouldn't get away with it. We've got a free press that asks questions – and those newspaper guys don't give up easy.'

'I think,' the girl said, 'that your president lied about your U.2. spy plane. Is it not so?'

Brogan looked a bit taken aback. 'That was an exception... Anyway, *he* didn't get away with it.'

Silence fell again. Presently Royce started on a new tack. 'What are your plans, Miss Lermontov, now that your friends are dead?'

'I shall wait here until the weather improves,' she said. 'Then the helicopter will pick me up.'

'Ah, yes... Have you plenty of food?'

'I have enough.'

'Have you a tent?'

'No – the tent was in one of the rucksacks that fell when the cornice broke. But I shall manage.'

'How?'

'I shall sleep in the open – it is not very cold. There is no frost and little wind. I have

113

done it many times before.'

'Have you got a good sleeping bag?'

'Of course. All our equipment is excellent.'

'I dare say the three of us could squeeze in here for the night, at a pinch.'

'Thank you, no.' The girl started to get up. 'I shall leave now.'

'At least let me make you some tea before you go,' Royce said. 'It'll only take a few minutes.'

'Thank you – but I have water to drink. Please do not concern yourself about me at all. Good-bye...'

Brogan rolled back the sleeve so that she could get out more easily. 'See you...!' She squeezed through the opening, picked up her sack and ice axe, and disappeared into the gloom.

'Well, what do you know!' Brogan said. 'There's a tough baby if ever I saw one!'

Royce nodded. 'Quite remarkable... Mind you, she may have been putting up a bit of a front for our benefit.'

'Think so? She didn't strike me as being overly distressed at the loss of her comrades.'

'That could have been an act, too... No emotion in the face of the enemy.'

'Maybe... Do you reckon she'll be okay out there?'

'She will if she's used to it. I've known a Sherpa spend a night under a blanket in a hard frost at sixteen thousand feet and be none the worse for it next day... Anyway, there's nothing we can do. You'd have had to get your gun out to make her stay.'

'That's a fact...' Brogan was silent for a moment. Then he said, 'By the way, Chief, I guess I owe you a word of thanks about that cornice. I had a pretty close shave myself, come to think of it.'

'Forget it,' Royce said.

Through the opening of the tent they watched the girl scraping out a flat place in the snow by the light of a dim torch, twenty yards along the ridge. She spent some time building up the snow into walls, to make a roofless shelter. Then the light went out and they lost sight of her.

After supper, Royce strolled through the murk to the top of the ridge. The girl was there, standing above the *couloir* as though she were keeping a vigil. Royce didn't speak to her.

11

During the night there was a small but welcome change in the weather. When Royce stuck his head out through the sleeve shortly after daybreak he saw that the cloud base had lifted. Banks of mist were still eddying around at ridge level, which meant that no helicopters could get through it, but below the ridge the view was clear. For the first time it would be possible to see down into the *couloir*. Royce reported the change. Brogan roused himself at once and began to pull on his boots. Royce went outside. The snow was still soft underfoot, the temperature a degree or two above freezing. He took a few steps towards the girl's snow shelter, wondering how she'd fared. She was lying asleep on the ground between the white mounds she'd built up, swathed in her bulky clothes and sleeping sack, her face almost covered by the ear flaps and turned-down peak of her fur hat. He left her undisturbed and took a couple of turns round the camp, getting his circulation going.

In a few minutes Brogan joined him. Together they climbed the ridge, following the skid track of the plane for easier walking, picking their way through the scattered debris of the wreck, now almost hidden by snow, and coming out once more at the spot where the cornice had broken off. They stood there, gazing out. At last there was something to look at besides cloud. Away to the north, snow-clad mountains stretched away in range after range – the mountains of Soviet Armenia. Nearer to them, in a high valley, they could make out some white houses, a long straight road, a building that looked like a factory. And, immediately beneath them, the great gully into which the plane fuselage had fallen. They concentrated on that.

The *couloir* was a wild-looking place – a deep, V-shaped rent in the mountain, its rocky walls almost sheer. The head of the V, where the floor of the *couloir* reached the mountain face, was choked with great mounds of snow and ice that had been worn and pressured into fantastic shapes. The edges of the huge mass had shrunk away from the embracing arms of rock on either side and it hung precariously over a steep, stony moraine. Below the moraine there was a vertiginous plunge down the north wall of the mountain.

Brogan was the first to spot the fuselage. Holed and broken-backed, it was lying half-buried in the snow and ice that had fallen with it. It had been carried out over the moraine and had come to rest against a pro-truding rock, a hundred feet below them and about eighty feet out from the *couloir's* eastern wall.

Royce focused his binoculars on it. Through the break at its centre he could see right into the interior. There was something inside that looked like a body. That would be one of the crew. Outside, a man's arm was sticking up vertically out of the snow. An arm in a grey-green padded sleeve. One of the Russian climbers. There was no sign of the other one. Wherever he was, he was undoubtedly dead.

Royce passed the glasses to Brogan without comment. There was a long silence while Brogan made his own inspection.

'Well?' Royce said at last.

Brogan gave a faint shrug. 'I guess I've still got work to do.'

'You think there could be anything worth while left of the camera after two crashes?'

'Sure, there could. Enough to show the Russkies how the thing was put together... If the whole lot had gone over the edge, that would have been that. But it hasn't. It's still within reach and I'll have to do what I came for.'

Royce gazed down at the mass of snow and ice suspended above the *couloir*. 'That stuff looks as though it would move at a touch,' he said. 'It's ripe, like the cornice.'

Brogan nodded. 'I'm not arguing, Chief. You were right yesterday and I guess you're right to-day... It's a chance I'll have to take.'

'If you set off an explosion,' Royce said, 'it won't be just a chance – it'll be a certainty. And once a fall starts there's no telling where it'll end. The whole *couloir* could be swept bare.'

'That's right – so I'll have to keep well out of the way! I've no choice, bud – I can't quit. My orders were to destroy the camera *at all costs.*'

118

Royce looked hard at him. 'I didn't know that. If I *had* known, I'm not sure I'd have agreed to lead you.'

Brogan grinned. 'Maybe that's why nobody told you!'

'You realise, of course, that what's left of the fuselage is on Russian soil now? We've no legal right to go down there.'

'Legality didn't bother the Russkies too much when they climbed up here,' Brogan said. 'So it's not going to bother me.'

'Our friend from the Turkish Foreign Office, Kilchuk, wouldn't approve. He was all for legality.'

'Maybe,' Brogan said. 'But he wasn't the guy that gave me the orders!'

Royce was silent for a while. Then he said, 'Wouldn't it be just as good if you set off your explosive at the top of the *couloir*, without going down there? The snow would avalanche, and carry the fuselage away. And it would probably be buried for ever.'

'What if the snow didn't avalanche? I'd have lost my chance.'

'I can practically guarantee that it will.'

Brogan shook his head. 'We still couldn't be sure the fuselage would be buried. The Russkies might find it and pick up the pieces – and one of the pieces might be the camera... Sorry, Chief, but my mind's made up. I'm going to *see* that camera smashed.'

With a sigh, Royce abandoned the struggle.

'All right. If that's how you feel I suppose there's nothing more to be said... How are you going to tackle the job?'

'Well,' Brogan said, 'the descent won't be any problem – if I use two ropes tied together I can rope down all the way. I'll have to rely on the ice axes for an anchor, and hope for the best. Once I'm down I'll fix the charge and take the wire back behind that big black rock under the east wall...' He pointed. 'No snow slide is going to shift that.'

'How much wire have you got?'

'A hundred feet – more than ample.'

Royce nodded. 'You'll have quite a job climbing back.'

Brogan turned the glasses on the east wall. 'I don't reckon so – it looks pretty broken to me. There should be plenty of holds. With you belaying me at the top, it'll be a cinch.'

'M'm... Well, I still don't like it. Not any part of it.'

Brogan smiled wryly. 'You think *I* do...? Come on, let's go get some breakfast. We'll feel better with full bellies.'

They were back on the top of the ridge by nine o'clock. Brogan had checked over the demolition gear in his rucksack, put in slings and waist loop, and made sure he had pitons, hammer and rings in case he needed them for the climb up. All the rest of his stuff he'd left in the tent to save unnecessary weight. Royce uncoiled the long nylon rope and one of the spares and joined them with a fisherman's knot. 'Where are you planning to go down?' he asked.

'Right above the black rock,' Brogan said. 'I can take a look at the holds as I rope down, and I'll be all set for the return trip.'

Royce nodded and moved along the ridge till he had the rock below him. He poked the shaft of his ice axe experimentally into the snow. It went in with dangerous ease at first – and then struck hard ground with inches of the shaft still exposed.

'You'll never anchor safely in this stuff,' he said. 'It's soft and shallow. We'll have to find something better.' He started to excavate a trench in the snow with his axe, throwing aside the large lumps, working back from the edge. When he came to the rock floor he explored the surface with the point of his pick, feeling for a crack. He toiled for ten minutes and paused, sweating. For the first time since the start of the trip, there was a hint of sun behind the mist.

Brogan picked up his axe. 'Okay, I'll take over.'

'You save your strength,' Royce said. He applied himself again to his digging and scraping. Presently he gave a satisfied grunt as the point of the pick found a crack. He brushed the loose snow away from it and felt around it with his fingers. 'Just the job,' he said. He stuck a piton in, drove it home, fixed a snap ring, tested it, and stood back. 'Right, Captain – it's all yours. Are you going to hump your sack down, or lower it?'

'Might as well lower it,' Brogan said. He parked his ice axe in the loops, fixed a ring to the straps, and let the sack down over the edge on a doubled rope. It found a lodgement almost at the bottom, close to the black shelter rock. He hauled the rope back, threaded it through the piton ring on the ground, and pulled on the two ends till it was held by the ring at its middle.

'Well, I guess that's it,' he said. He glanced along the ridge. The girl had appeared and was sitting on her rucksack, fifty yards away, watching. 'Better keep an eye on Big Sister, in case she tries any tricks. Okay – see you, Chief!'

'Good luck!' Royce said.

Brogan grasped the doubled rope, passed it under one thigh and over one shoulder, and lowered himself backwards over the edge, his feet against the rock face.

Royce moved along the curve of the ridge to a point where he could watch the descent. Brogan was going down in a series of controlled swoops, checking himself by the grip of his gloved hand on the rope and braking with his body as he approached the bottom. In a few moments he was down. He retrieved his rucksack and backed away down the steep moraine, holding on to the rope and letting the anchor take his weight. As soon as he reached the fuselage he tied on his waist loop and made the rope fast to it. He was still on a slope, the precipice was only a few yards away, and he needed his hands free.

Royce glanced across at the girl. She had moved nearer to the edge of the *couloir* in order to see better what was going on. At fifty yards, her silent hostility was as cold as the mountain – but she showed no sign of trying to interfere. Royce switched his gaze back to the moraine, focusing his glasses on the fuselage. Brogan had entered it through the gaping hole at its centre, carrying his rucksack. Royce could just see him, moving around inside. He stayed there for what seemed an interminable time. Royce kept casting uneasy glances at the snow mass poised in the V of the *couloir.* There was no reason why it should start to slide at that moment, but it had to move some time. And the fuselage was right in its path...

At last! Brogan was coming out. He had the rucksack on his back, now, and a coil of wire in his hand. He signalled to Royce. Royce returned to the piton anchor and prepared to take in the slack of the rope. Brogan started to move backwards up the moraine towards the shelter rock, paying out the wire in front of him. Royce took the strain of his weight on the rope, keeping it taut without jerking, helping him along with a steady pull. Brogan was only twenty feet now from the shelter rock. Suddenly he stopped. He seemed to be in some sort of trouble. Royce turned the binoculars on him – and saw at once what the trouble was. There was no more wire!

Brogan cupped his hands and called up. 'Some son-of-a-bitch must have short-measured me!' He stood for a while, looking around, debating what to do. Then he started to retrace his steps down the slope, taking the end of the wire with him, heading for a big boulder away to his right. A tug on the rope jerked him to a stop and he turned and motioned to Royce to let out more slack.

Royce shouted down: 'It's not safe, Brogan. Don't be a fool. Come back!' He ran a loop of the rope through the piton ring to give him leverage and put all his weight on it, holding Brogan stationary.

There was a tense silence. Then Brogan called up, 'If you don't slacken off, I shall unrope.'

'*Wait…!*'

Brogan's hands went to his waist loop. He was beginning to untie the knot… Royce slackened off.

Helpless, now, he could only watch. Brogan slid down to the boulder. Crouching behind it, he took the battery from his sack. In seconds, he had the wire attached. He looked up at Royce – and waved.

There was a flash of flame from the fuse-lage as it disintegrated. Then sound and shock waves hit the *couloir*. Before the noise of the explosion had died, the teetering snow mass in the V began to slide. It gathered momentum, spreading out across the *couloir*, rolling up detritus in front of it, sweeping down towards the precipice with a roar like thunder. Brogan was on his feet, struggling to keep his balance against the shock wind, scrambling and clawing his way up the loose surface of the moraine towards the shelter rock. Royce kept the rope taut. It was all he could do.

Ten feet from the rock, Brogan slipped. The rope held him, but the fall cost him precious seconds. He recovered, and started off again, heaving on the rope, straining to get clear. Only five feet now to the rock! He was almost there! Then the edge of the avalanche caught him. He disappeared from view in a swirling hell of snow and ice and boulders – and the rope went slack.

CHAPTER III

THE DESCENT

Three hours had passed since Brogan's death. Three hours, for Royce, of mental turmoil.

He knew he couldn't have dissuaded Brogan from going down the *couloir*. He knew he couldn't have dissuaded him from using the short wire. He knew he had done all in his power to help him, once he was down there. Even so, as the leader and planner of the expedition he could hardly escape a share of the responsibility. He ought to have had that wire out and measured it – not taken its length on trust, when so much depended on it. He would never have taken the length of a rope on trust. By his own exacting standards, he had been negligent.

His personal distress was deep. He had liked Brogan; and though their acquaintance had been brief he felt an acute sense of loss. Three days of shared hardships and dangers had created a considerable bond, at least as far as he was concerned. He had enjoyed Brogan's companionship, respected him for his forthright integrity, enormously admired his courage. That final reckless act had been truly heroic and sacrificial – an act that Royce would remember with humility and vicarious pride.

Brogan had said he would never make the headlines – and as a climber perhaps he wouldn't have done. But he'd certainly make them now. Always supposing that Royce got back alive to tell the story – which at the moment was very far from sure...

He gazed unhappily out of the tent. The promise of the morning's weather had not been fulfilled. The cloud had thickened again and was much lower down on the ridge. It looked as though the forecast of the met. men was going to prove right. In that case, the prospects would be grim. With deep foreboding, Royce contemplated the choices and the chances. If the helicopter failed to get through in the next day or two, he would be faced with hazards far more desperate than any he had known so far. Hazards that at the moment he could see no way of overcoming. Unless...

His thoughts turned to the girl. Since the loss of her companions, her situation had been basically the same as the one he faced now. Was she worried about it? Perhaps she didn't realise that the weather was likely to remain bad... He wondered what had happened to her. At some point in the appalling moments that had followed the avalanche he had lost sight of her. She had gone off without a word – demonstrating, no doubt, her condemnation of the act she'd witnessed, her determination to stay aloof... But she couldn't go on wandering about in the mist for ever. She'd be back...

Meanwhile, he could only wait and occupy himself as best he could. He sorted out the gear that Brogan had left in the tent, putting the food and spare pitons and anything else that might be useful to him in his own rucksack. He unknotted and coiled the nylon ropes he had retrieved after the disaster, inspected them for damage, and sealed the broken ends in a candle flame. Not that the ends were much frayed. They had been cut cleanly through by ice, as though by a sharp knife...

It was shortly before one o'clock when the girl appeared again out of the mist. She made straight for her snow shelter and for some minutes was obscured by its high walls. Then she emerged and set off at a brisk plod up the ridge. This time she had her rucksack at her back and rope slung over her shoulder. She was carrying her ice axe.

Royce watched her, frowning. She was heading very purposefully for the *couloir*. Too purposefully...! After a moment he left the tent and climbed to the rim. The girl was peering down, studying the rock face.

He joined her. 'What are you planning to do?' he asked.

She regarded him coldly. 'What does it look like? Obviously I am about to descend.'

'You said you were going to wait for a helicopter.'

'Yes, but I have changed my mind. I have decided to return now.'

'Then you must be crazy,' Royce said. 'You'll never make it.'

'It is nothing to do with you.'

'It's something to do with me if I have to watch another fatality on the mountain. You haven't a chance. You might just as well throw yourself over the edge and be done with it.'

'I do not think so.'

'Then you've no judgment and you oughtn't to be climbing at all. You know the state of the rock – it's icy and slippery. A lot of the holds are crumbling away. Almost every pitch is a severe hazard... We had two bad falls on the way up, as well as several near misses. If I hadn't been roped I'd be dead. I'm sure your party must have had falls too.'

The girl looked at him sullenly. Her face, under its outdoor tan, was pale and strained. 'Very few,' she said.

'How many do you need, for God's sake? Isn't one enough, if you're not belayed...? I tell you it's suicide.'

'It is always possible to rope down.'

'Rope down three thousand feet – on your

own! What happens when you run out of pitons and rings? What happens when your rope jams above an overhang? What happens when you've descended two or three pitches without holds, and you look below for the next stance and there isn't one? You can't go on and you can't go back. So you cling there in the cold and die miserably... Really, you're talking like a novice.'

The girl's eyes flashed. 'I am far from being a novice. On the contrary, I am a Master of Sport.'

'Oh? And what precisely does that mean?'

'It means that I am one of the best climbers in the Soviet Union. It means that I have done many 5B climbs, the most severe. It means that I have done high altitude climbs in the Pamirs and the Tian Shan. It means that I am an expert of experts – and you try to teach me! What have you done that is comparable?'

Royce shrugged. 'I have led expeditions. In the Antarctic, in Greenland, in the Himalaya.'

The girl stared at him. 'Is that true?'

'Certainly it's true. Why shouldn't it be?'

'What is your name?'

'My name's Royce.'

'Not – *William* Royce?'

'That's right.'

For a moment the girl continued to stare. Then she said, 'Yes – now I recognise your face. I have seen it in books. At first I did not realise...'

'A three-day beard doesn't help,' Royce said.

'No...' The girl seemed unable to take her eyes from his. 'I hardly know what to say. I have read all your mountain books, in English. I have studied your climbs, your expeditions. I have greatly admired your achievements. In any other circumstances, I would have considered it a very great honour to meet you. You are an exceptional man.'

'If you believe that,' Royce said, 'perhaps you'll accept my advice about climbing down alone.'

The girl gave a hard little laugh. 'Your advice was good – but it was not necessary. Of course I know that to descend alone in these conditions is madness. I think that probably I shall be killed. But there is a small chance – and I must take it. I have no choice.'

'Why have you no choice?'

'Because of the weather. I hoped it would improve, and that soon the helicopter would come. So to-day I waited. But now I see that the cloud is coming down again – and I cannot wait. I must go now, while I still have strength... You see – I have no food.'

'No food!'

'None. All the food of my party was in the rucksacks on the cornice. All of it was lost.'

131

'You mean you haven't eaten anything since the cornice fell?'

'No.'

It was Royce who stared now. 'Why on earth didn't you tell us? We would gladly have given you some of ours.'

'I did not want your food. I did not wish to take anything from the enemies of my country.'

'You're incredible.'

'I am Russian. To be Russian is to be proud.'

'I admire your pride,' Royce said. 'I respect your feelings. All the same, I do beg you now to share my food. I've got plenty – and after what you've told me it would choke me to eat it alone. If you refuse, and climb down, and fall, I shall feel responsible.'

The girl was silent.

Royce said, 'Up here, Miss Lermontov, it's the mountains that are our opponents, not other climbers. You should know that. I ask you not as an Englishman, but as one climber to another. If our positions were reversed I'd expect you to help me. So let me help you. Come to the tent, and eat, and talk. To-morrow, when you're strong again, you can decide what to do. You won't have lost anything.'

For a moment the girl hesitated. Then, with great dignity, she said, 'Very well… Because you are William Royce, and you ask me as a fellow climber, I will accept. Thank you…'

Royce lit the petrol stove and took out one ration of food from his rucksack. The girl handed him the melting-pot of clean snow she'd gathered, and he put it on the stand.

'It'll take a little time to make the hoosh,' he said. 'You'd better have something to be going on with.' He opened the ration and passed her its contents of biscuits, butter and cheese.

She took them gratefully. 'You are very kind… And I am very hungry.' She began to eat.

Royce said, 'What other names have you besides Lermontov?'

'My first name is Varvara,' she told him. 'My patronymic is Mikhailovna. My friends call me Varya.'

'May I call you Varya?'

The girl's face softened in a smile. 'With my mouth full of your food, how can I refuse? And it will be simpler.'

Royce nodded.

Varya said, 'Why do you not eat too?'

'I'm not particularly hungry.'

'You are sad for your friend, I think.'

'Yes – very.'

'What was he called?'

'Brogan. Captain Gene Brogan, of the United States Army.'

'He was a brave man. I cannot deny that,

133

even though he was an enemy. I think he knew what would happen.'

'Yes... He also knew what he was doing and why.'

There was a little silence. Then Varya said, 'Do *you* believe that the aeroplane was stolen from Germany by a Soviet agent, because of its camera?'

'It's not a question of belief,' Royce said. 'I know.'

'*How* do you know? After all, you were not there. You did not see.'

'I know because I was told by people I trust.'

'Is that a good reason? I was told a different story – by people *I* trust. Why should your version be right, and mine wrong?'

'Answering that,' Royce said, 'would start us off on a big argument.'

'Does that matter? We have plenty of time.'

'I dare say – but a fierce argument wouldn't help us to digest the hoosh.'

'It would not be fierce, since I am your guest... Perhaps you do not wish to argue because you know your case is bad.'

'That's not it at all,' Royce said. 'It's simply that I doubt if we'd find any common ground – therefore we wouldn't get anywhere. As an interpreter for the Russian Foreign Ministry, you wouldn't be in the least likely to agree with me. I'm sure you've been well indoctrinated.'

'If you mean that I am a good Communist...'

'Yes, that's what I mean.'

'Then it is true, and I am glad of it. It is to communism that the future belongs.'

Royce shrugged. 'That remains to be seen, doesn't it?'

'You think that your capitalist democracy is perfect and will last for ever?'

'Not at all,' Royce said. 'No system of government lasts for ever. And democracy is a very fragile growth – it needs the right conditions to flourish. Conditions that aren't often found... It's certainly not perfect, either. But it's a very precious thing to those of us who have it – and a great deal better than tyranny.'

'Is not your imperialism a tyranny?'

'You mean to-day...? We lost our empire, you know.'

'But not willingly. You would have retained it if it had not been wrested from you by struggle.'

Royce gave the hoosh a stir. 'That's not entirely true. I think we lost the will to keep it... Anyhow, it's gone.'

'And that is a good thing,' Varya said. 'What suffering you caused before it went! Your oppressions, your colonial wars, your gunboats. I have read about these things. Even recently, your Suez...'

Royce shrugged again. The discussion was,

inevitably, covering well-worn ground. 'I'm not pretending that the British Empire was built up on milk and honey and kindness,' he said. 'But all countries, in their time, are guilty of aggression, cruelties, mistakes. *All* of us... Do you know that English saying about the pot calling the kettle black?'

'I have heard it... It means, I think, that one should not criticise others for faults one has oneself.'

'Exactly... The Soviet Union, after all, has by far the greatest empire in the world to-day. Most of it consists of subject territories that you conquered – in Asia, and in Europe.'

Varya shook her head. 'You do not understand. At first they may have been conquered – but when the Revolution came they remained with us because they wished to. Because the people did not want any longer to be exploited by landlords and capitalists.'

'Were the people asked, do you suppose?'

'There was never any question. They welcomed us with open arms, because we brought freedom from oppression... And this we shall continue to do.'

'I don't doubt it,' Royce said. 'Communism's an aggressive philosophy – always looking around to see where it can stir up trouble.'

'Where there is evil in the world, it is necessary to stir up trouble.'

'That depends on the nature of the evil,'

Royce said. 'And on the motives of the stirrers…!'

There was a little pause. Then Varya said, 'At least you are right about one thing. We shall never agree.'

'No.'

'And – to go back to where we started – when you say that your story of the aeroplane is right, and mine wrong, that is just prejudice. You are simply against my country.'

'Not your country,' Royce said. 'Your government.'

'All right – my government. But it is still prejudice. You have produced not a single practical argument.'

'Well,' Royce said, 'let me put this practical question to you. If the aeroplane wasn't testing a secret camera over Germany, as I maintain, but was sent into Russia to take spy photographs, as you maintain, why should Brogan have sacrificed himself to destroy the camera? What would have been his purpose?'

'I think the answer to that is simple. It *was* a spy camera – but also of a new and secret type which he did not wish should fall into our hands.'

Royce gave a wintry smile. 'Your logic's all right… It's just your facts that are wrong.'

Varya put down her plastic cup with a sigh of contentment. She had eaten most of the hoosh and all the chocolate, and drunk about a pint of hot, sweet tea. 'That was wonderful,' she said. 'I feel much better now.'

Royce nodded. 'You look much better.'

She glanced out of the tent. 'The cloud has come down farther.'

'Yes,' Royce said. 'I'm afraid the prospects aren't at all good.'

'Were you also expecting a helicopter to pick you up?'

'Only if the weather improved – and I was warned that it probably wouldn't for some days. Brogan and I were planning to climb down together, to-morrow. Now that he's dead, I face the same problem as you do.'

Varya looked at him in surprise. 'I see no problem for you. If you have plenty of food, you can afford to wait.'

Royce groped for his pipe and began to fill it, avoiding her eye. 'I've a confession to make,' he said. 'I've food for two people for one more day. That's all.'

Varya stared. 'But you told me...'

'I know I did. I had to, to stop you climbing down.'

'Then I am very sorry. You have put me too much in your debt... Now I feel terrible.'

There's no reason why you should,' Royce said. 'I was thinking of myself quite as much as of you. You see – I need you. As much as you need me.'

'What do you mean?'

'It's quite simple. I don't believe the

138

weather's going to improve. I think we're going to have this cloud for some time yet. If we stay here, hoping for a change, hoping that the helicopters will come, and they don't, we shall run out of food and fuel and very soon we'll be too weak to move and we'll die of hunger and exposure. If we try to climb down separately, it's almost certain we'll both be killed. That leaves only one thing. If we want to survive, we must climb down together.'

Varya looked slightly taken aback. For a while she sat thinking about it, frowning. Then she nodded. 'What you say, of course, is sensible. It is the only way to be sure. And I would enjoy descending with you – it would be an experience I would value. Yes – it is an excellent idea... So you will come down into my country?'

Royce shook his head. 'I'm afraid that's impossible.'

'Why?'

'Because I've no desire to spend the rest of my life in a Soviet labour camp. Directly we got down, your security people would want to know what had happened about the aeroplane. As a loyal Soviet citizen, you'd naturally tell them everything. And I'd be arrested. Technically, I've assisted in an act of sabotage on Soviet soil. I wouldn't have a chance.'

'I am sure our authorities would not wish to arrest William Royce.'

'I don't share your certainty,' Royce said. 'Anyhow, it's a risk I'm not prepared to take.'

'You are suggesting, then, that I should descend on your side of the mountain?'

'Yes.'

'But I too could be arrested.'

'For what?'

'For crossing the Turkish border illegally to help remove something which your people say my country stole. Is that not enough?'

'I'm sure no one would bother about that,' Royce said. 'Whatever your intentions may have been, the fact is that you didn't do a thing. And now that the camera's destroyed, no one would want to make any more trouble. You'd be quite safe.'

'You think you can speak with authority for the Turks? And the Americans?'

'In this case I'm sure I can. The Turks are most anxious to remain on good terms with your country – they'll be only too glad to let the matter drop. And the Americans have got what they wanted – why should they worry...? As a matter of fact you'd probably be treated as a heroine – for saving my life by agreeing to climb down with me. You'd find everyone very friendly – and you'd be free to fly back to Russia whenever you wished.'

'That is what you believe. You cannot know.'

'I do know,' Royce said. 'But if you're

going to feel anxious about it, I'll give you an undertaking. I'll say nothing that could possibly result in your being accused of any offence, till you're safely out. That's a promise. If necessary I'll lie in my teeth – I'll say the cornice collapsed of its own accord and that your party never crossed the border. Till you're safe.'

'Such promises cannot always be kept. Under interrogation, you might weaken.'

'What interrogation? I shan't be interrogated – not in the way you mean. We don't go in for bright lights and beatings. You mustn't judge us by yourselves.'

'I do not believe that the security police in the West are so kind and humane.'

'You don't have to believe it. The situation just won't arise. All that will happen is that I shall have a friendly word with the people who asked me to accompany Brogan, tell them the task was carried out, explain that you climbed down with me at my request, and say you'd like to leave. In twenty-four hours, you'll be out. I guarantee it.'

Varya looked at him uncertainly. 'Well,' she said, 'I will think about it.'

At Royce's suggestion they went for a brief slog along the ridge while there was a little daylight left. Conditions were far from pleasant in the dank cloud, but they managed to work up a glow and felt better for the exercise. As dusk fell they returned to the tent and settled down there for the long evening ahead.

Neither of them referred again to the question of what they would do next day. Instead, they began to talk of each other.

Royce said, 'Do you live alone in Moscow?'

Varya nodded. 'Until three years ago I lived with my parents. We had two large rooms in the Arbat. Then they left to work in the provinces – but I was allowed to keep both rooms. I am very privileged.'

'Have you always had your home there?'

'No – I was brought up in the Ukraine. My father is a Cossack, from the valley of the Don.'

'The river that flows quietly.'

'Yes. The river, I would say, is quieter than the Cossacks. They have the reputation of being a fierce and independent people.'

'Now that I've met one,' Royce said, 'I can see why.'

Varya smiled. 'My great-grandfather was very fierce. For a little time there was a picture of him in our house, in his uniform, with a big moustache and a sabre. He was an officer in the Tsarist cavalry and was killed at the battle of Tannenberg. My father also fought, in the Great Patriotic War against the Nazis, and was decorated... My mother is quite different – she is very gentle. Her family were professional people, who came from Leningrad.'

'What do your parents do?'

'My mother is now a teacher in Irkutsk. My father is an engineer in Alma Ata.'

'So I suppose you don't see much of them?'

'I have seen my father once since he left – that is all. My mother not at all. It is like that in the Soviet Union – the country is so big, and families often become separated because of their work. But it is necessary to go where one is needed – and if one is a Party member it is an obligation.'

'Are you a Party member?'

'Not yet, but I hope to be.'

Royce nodded. 'I have a feeling you'll make it... Tell me, how do you manage to climb so much, if you've got a regular job as an interpreter?'

'I am often given leave. To be a Master of Sport is considered an important job in itself. I have to keep up my training so that I can train others.'

'Where do you train? There aren't any hills near Moscow, are there?'

'Not climbing hills. We practise sometimes on the walls of a ruined monastery – but that is mainly for amusement. In the summer we have camps in the Caucasus – there are many of them, run by our trade unions. That is a very healthy and vigorous life. We are wakened early by loudspeakers and do physical drill before breakfast. Also we play basket ball, and exercise on parallel bars. And of course we undertake many expeditions. As a Master of Sport I can choose my own climbs, as long as the camp commandant gives his approval.'

'You mean you can't just go off as you please?'

'Naturally there must be organisation. Each time, before I leave, I must fill in a form showing the details of the intended climb.'

'Really? What details?'

'Well, how many are to be in the party, and what food and equipment we are taking and which route we are following. This makes it easier for rescue, in case we get into difficulties.'

'Yes,' Royce said. 'I can see the advantages…'

'It is a good arrangement – it has saved many lives… Then, on our return, there is always a little ceremony. We form into line, and the camp commandant asks us if we have successfully performed our mission. If the answer is yes, the onlookers give three cheers and we are presented with flowers.'

'Very nice. And what are you presented with it your mission is not successfully performed?'

'Ah – then there have to be explanations. If a big error has been made, a Master may have his badge taken away.'

'I see,' Royce said. 'Well, we all have our

144

different customs...'

There was a little silence. Then Varya said, 'Now, please, tell me something about yourself. Where do you live, when you are not climbing?'

'I've an apartment in a city called Cambridge,' Royce told her. 'That's the home of one of our great universities. I live in a close – a private precinct of the university. It's very old and beautiful and quiet, with no traffic, and there's a lawn just outside my door where I can stroll, and you can see the river through an archway.'

'It sounds very peaceful,' Varya said. 'I think you are fortunate to have such a place.'

'I am,' Royce agreed. 'Especially as I leave it empty so much. It'll be months before I see it again.'

'What are you engaged in now?'

'I'm on my way to India.' Royce told her about his climbing plans, and the van journey he was going to make. 'It should be quite a trip,' he said. 'We go through Syria and Jordan, then we have about six hundred miles of desert to Baghdad, and afterwards we cross Persia, which'll probably be the toughest of the lot. But it should be an interesting journey – there'll be high mountain passes, sandstorms, sheikhs, camels, nomads, floods, mud – just about everything, I imagine.'

'I envy you,' Varya said. 'I would very much like to see such places. I have always wished to travel.'

'Perhaps you will, some day. Doesn't the Soviet Union ever send its climbers on expeditions to other parts of the world?'

'It does, but not very often... However, I shall hope.'

'At least,' Royce said, 'you have seen things in your own country that I never shall. Tell me about some of those high altitude climbs you did. I've always been interested in the Pamirs...'

They chatted on, telling their stories, discussing climbing technicalities, absorbed now in their common interest. It was Royce who, in the end, said they must eat again; Royce who, after the frugal meal, brought the evening's talk to a conclusion.

'Whatever you may decide to do to-morrow,' he said, 'it's obvious that we're both of us in for a very strenuous time. I think we should turn in.' He looked quizzically at Varya. 'Do you want to go out into the cold and sleep in your snow bed again?'

'Do you wish me to?' she asked.

'Of course not. I think it would be absurd – there's plenty of room for both of us here. And I feel in need of company.'

Varya nodded gravely. 'In that case,' she said, 'I will stay.'

2

Royce's first waking moments next morning were moments of shock.

Some time, in the pre-dawn light, he had been aware of a stirring at his side, of Varya leaving the tent. He had assumed she would be back, and had dropped asleep again. It was only when he came to full consciousness and looked around that he saw she hadn't returned. Not only that, but the rucksack she'd used for a pillow had gone, too.

He snatched up his boots, pulled them on, and went quickly outside. The cloud was thicker than ever. Visibility was no more than twenty paces. He looked to see if Varya's ice axe was still thrust into the snow beside his own. It wasn't.

He gazed blankly around. It seemed unbelievable that after all their talk about the dangers, the girl should have set off to climb down the mountain alone – and in such daunting weather. Even more unbelievable that after their friendly evening together she should have left without a word. But there was no sign or sound of her. He shouted 'Varya!' and stood listening. There was no reply. Whatever the reasons that had prompted her, she had gone.

Grim-faced, he climbed the slope to the top

of the ridge. The *couloir* was a cauldron of billowing cloud. He listened again, and could hear nothing. Once more he shouted 'Varya!' – though he hardly expected a reply. She'd been gone for at least half an hour and was probably well out of earshot. In any case, now that she'd started, she'd never come back. He stood there, gazing down, thinking sombrely of her prospects – and of his own.

The stark choice he'd put before Varya now confronted him alone. He could wait in that lifeless solitude, hoping for rescue, gambling on a change in the weather. Now that he was on his own he had food and fuel for perhaps two days. But once his supplies were finished, it wouldn't take long for his resistance to weaken and his body to cool. He'd face a long-drawn-out, miserable end in loneliness and desolation. At least the alternative would be quicker. The first jammed rope, the first slip on those icy rocks, would finish him. But the alternative offered not even a hope. It wasn't going to be an easy choice…

He turned, and began to retrace his steps through the soft snow. As he drew near the tent, a figure emerged from the mist. Varya, rucksack on back and ice axe in hand, plodding up the slope from the south side.

'Good morning!' she said cheerfully.

He gazed at her in anger and relief. 'Where on earth have you been?'

'I went to see if there was any thinning of

the cloud farther down,' she said. 'A short reconnaissance.'

'I wish you'd told me.'

'I am sorry. You were sleeping – I did not want to disturb you.'

'Didn't you hear me calling?'

'No, I heard nothing.'

'I've been very worried. I thought you'd gone for good.'

She looked at him in hurt surprise. 'I would not have done that without telling you. How could you think it?'

Royce grunted. 'Well, it's over now... Anyway, what did you find?'

'The cloud is much lower than it was. I think it continues far down the face.'

'So what have you decided to do?'

'What choice have I? There will be no helicopter to-day, that is certain. And to climb down alone would be more stupid to-day even than yesterday. So if you will not come with me, I must go with you – and trust in what you promised.'

'You can safely do that,' Royce said. 'And I'm sure you won't regret your decision... Right, let's have something to eat and get started. Even with the two of us, it's going to be a long, hard struggle.'

In less than an hour they had breakfasted, refilled their water bottles with melted snow, packed up the tent and their belongings and put on their crampons. As they roped up Varya asked, 'Will we climb down by the route you ascended?'

'I'm afraid not,' Royce said. 'An ice slope broke up when Brogan and I crossed it. We'll have to find a new way.' He took a compass bearing and pointed to the south-east. 'In that direction for a start. Ready?'

'Yes, I am ready.'

'Off you go, then – and take it gently. Remember that most accidents happen on the way down! And keep the pitches as short as you can when we get to the face...'

They set off down the southern slope of the ridge. Royce, as the stronger climber, now occupied the rear position on the rope, the more responsible and hazardous in a descent. At first they ploughed over the tracks that Varya had made in her sortie that morning. Then they swung to the left on to virgin snow. The going was very soft. Royce guessed that the temperature was still a few degrees above freezing, though the envelop-ing cloud made it feel colder.

Gradually the slope steepened. The sharp angle called for special care in the mist and Royce held himself ready for an instant ice-axe belay in case of need. But Varya moved down sure-footedly, zigzagging when they came to a sheet of slippery snow-ice and cut-ting steps with a few expert strokes as they dropped abruptly to the edge of the precipitous face. They paused there for a moment while Royce drove in a piton and anchored. Then Varya lowered herself over the side, found a toehold, and started to descend.

For the first few pitches Royce watched her closely, as in the earlier stages of the ascent he'd watched Brogan – appraising her footwork and her ropework, the way she distributed her weight, her choice of stances, the soundness of her belaying. As with Brogan, he soon ceased to worry. The girl had clearly earned her Master's badge. She moved with a technical skill and confidence and easy grace which, even in the anxious circumstances of their descent, Royce took pleasure in watching.

The climb down, always the more difficult half of the mountaineer's art, presented its own special problems, quite apart from the hazards of the weather. On the ascent it had been possible to study the rock above, to pick good holds and promising routes. Descending, it was much harder to see the holds below, and the venturing foot was often the only guide. Most of the pitches were too steep and severe for anything but a face-to-the-rock position, which gave little scope for prospecting. In the thick cloud, it was impossible to guess whether a pitch below would 'go' or not. The shortage of good stances was a continual worry. Occasionally, when a lower ledge was in sight and well-positioned, Varya would go down on her doubled spare rope, releasing it with a flick from its knob of rock when she was safely on the stance. Whenever possible, Royce did the same. But with the cloud cutting visibility to little more than twenty feet there were few opportunities to rope down without the risk of being caught on a holdless slab without a stance in view; and they used the method with caution. Mostly it was a question of step-by-step progress, of feeling the way with toe and finger, of tentative advances and time-wasting traverses and frequent retreats.

Varya had the harder task, since she was the pathfinder. But at least she could move in safety, securely belayed from above on a near-taut rope that would hold her against any slip. Royce, following her, faced some hair-raising hazards. Where the run-out to the next stance was a long one, he had to climb down knowing that Varya's belay, far below and out of sight, would do him no good if he fell free. Almost certainly the rope would break. He moved, on these occasions, with infinite care, testing each foothold, protecting his feet with tested handholds, always seeking to have three extremities on good holds at the same time, keeping his body as close as possible to the rock so that he could get an instantaneous friction grip if anything gave way. These were nightmare passages, a mountaineering folly, as he well knew. But with only a tiny ration of food left, and nearly three thousand feet of face to descend, the risks had to be taken.

They halted at noon on a rock platform that provided close-standing room above a sheer drop, and refreshed themselves with water from their bottles and a small portion of the day's food ration. They had climbed down, Royce guessed, perhaps five hundred feet – though with the cloud still hiding everything it was hard to judge distance accurately.

Varya, chewing with relish on biscuits and cheese, said, 'That was a most enjoyable descent.' She looked fresh and relaxed after her arduous morning. Her face, under the round fur hat, was rosy with health and exertion, her eyes sparkling with the pleasure of achievement. 'I like climbing with you.'

Royce smiled. 'I think you just like climbing.'

'No – with you everything is better. All the time, I feel in harmony with you. We move with the same rhythm. We suit each other. Do you not agree?'

'I agree,' Royce said.

'And always, I have complete faith. You are so cool, so careful – especially when you are obliged to take great risks. When you are climbing down above me, I have no fear – even when you are a long way away, even though I know a fall would tear me from my stance. I have such faith, I could sit and read a book until you came. Is that foolish?'

'It's a great compliment,' Royce said, 'which I'm happy to return. I trust you, too. You're a wonderful climber, Varya – one of the best I've ever known. I can think of no situation in which I wouldn't have absolute confidence in you.'

'You mean, of course, no *climbing* situation.'

'Well, yes…'

'Even with that limitation, I am flattered. When we get down I think I will ask you to write what you have said– "You are a wonderful climber, Varya" – and sign it "William Royce". Then I will take it back to the Soviet Union and show it to all the Honoured Masters of Sport, who are even better than I am – and I will treasure it.'

Royce laughed. 'It sounds to me like the start of a personality cult – you'd better watch it…! And you seem to have forgotten that I'm an enemy of your country!' He humped his sack. 'Right – let's get moving.'

They had been going for only a few minutes when they ran into trouble – of a kind they hadn't experienced before on the descent. There was a rumble overhead, and a shower of small boulders and flying fragments shot past them like cannon balls. They flattened themselves against the face, making the target as small as possible, and waited helplessly for the bombardment to end. Neither of them was hit by anything more than small pieces of ice and rubble, but it had been a narrow escape, and for some time afterwards their attention was directed as much to the rock above them as the rock below.

The landslip was followed by a succession of difficulties. They were turned by a long vertical slab without holds and had to make a slow and tiring traverse to the east before they could resume the descent. After two or three more pitches, in cloud that showed little sign of thinning, they realised they had strayed from the south face. They were going down into another big *couloir*, which Royce thought must be the one he'd noticed when he'd first examined the mountain through glasses. At the bottom there was a *bergschrund* – a deep fissure where an ice-and-snow bed had retreated from the rock wall. At first it looked as though they would be unable to cross it. There were a few places where the gap was closed, but only by treacherous, rotting snow that Royce refused to venture on. They made a long detour, looking for a safe bridge. Eventually they found one, at a spot that was permanently shaded by a high ice mound. They crossed it, and worked their way down through a chaotic ice fall, coming out at last on a snow-covered glacier.

Royce called a halt there and gazed doubtfully ahead. In the past few days he had, of necessity, broken almost every basic rule in the climbing book, and there was nothing particularly sacrosanct about the one that said 'Never go two on a glacier.' All the same, he hesitated. The glacier was sure to be crevassed – and some of the crevasses would have thin snow roofs, softened by the recent rise in temperature. Because of the weather, he had had no chance to study the glacier from above, to unravel its system and choose the best route through its complexities. With low visibility, and the cloud and snow surface merging in an almost uniform grey, it would be difficult to pick out the usual warning signs as they advanced. The prospect was as uninviting as any Royce had known.

He looked at Varya. 'Well – what do you think? Do we go on – or do we go back?'

She prodded the soft snow with her axe. 'It looks bad. But back to where?'

'That's just it,' Royce said. He stood considering. They had, perhaps, four hours of daylight left. If they retraced their steps up the *couloir*, they would still have to find an alternative to the slab that had turned them. The retreat could easily last till dusk. Then the morning would find them without food or fuel, and with three-quarters of the face still to be mastered. If, on the other hand, they followed the glacier down and didn't run into any bad trouble, they might well have half the mountain behind them by nightfall.

'I think we must go on,' he said finally. 'I don't like it – but we've a fair chance of getting through if we take proper precautions.'

Varya nodded. 'I also think we should try.'

'All right. We'll use my hundred-and-fifty-foot length of nylon full, with thirty feet between us. That'll be enough to save you being dragged down if I go through, and it'll just about allow us to keep each other in sight. We'll be left with a sixty-foot spare coil each, which we can use for possible rescue work.'

'I understand,' Varya said.

'Then let's switch over.'

They unroped, and tied on again to the new rope. Royce took from his rucksack the four circles of spliced hemp he'd brought with him – the Prusik slings. He passed two of them to Varya. 'You know how to use these?'

'Of course,' she said.

He watched her attach them to the climbing rope with the special knot that would hold fast under tension and slide when the sling was slack. One of the slings she kept near her body, it's loose end passed through her waist loop and tucked into a pocket. The other she pushed along the rope until its free end was comfortably within her grasp.

'That's fine!' Royce said. He fixed the other two slings to his own end of the rope

157

in the same way. 'Right – you know the drill. Watch me all the time. Don't let the rope go slack. Have your axe ready for a quick belay. Follow exactly in my tracks. And if I do go through, send down a bight of rope from your spare coil. I shall clip it on to my waist snap ring, and if you make an end fast to the axe and haul on the other it'll be as good as a single-block pulley and you'll be able to give me quite a bit of help. Okay?'

Varya nodded. Royce gave her cheek an affectionate pat, grasped his ice axe firmly by the head, and set off through the murk.

He moved slowly, probing with the point of the axe before he risked a step, testing the grip of the snow as the shaft went deeper. A satisfactory probe was no absolute guarantee that the surface would bear his weight, but a bad one would give clear warning. Every few yards he stopped and gazed around, trying to spot the telltale crevasse shadows, the hollows that told of weakness, the cracks on either side of him that might continue under his feet. But, as he'd expected, his knowledge of glacier signs was of little use to-day. What he could see through the cloud was minimal.

He plodded on, threading his way between ice hummocks, making detours round wide ice fissures, leaping across narrow ones, changing his course whenever the thrust of his ice axe raised a doubt, occasionally referring to the compass for his general direction. From time to time he looked back to see how Varya was faring. He had very little anxiety on her account – if the snow would bear his weight, it should bear hers. And she was following in his steps with the utmost concentration, watching him all the time, halting and bracing when he checked, letting out the necessary amount of rope when he had to jump, but otherwise keeping it just less than taut. He saw that she was holding a short coil in her right hand, with her ice axe already passed through it for an instant shaft belay. She was, he thought, a paragon of a climber. As well as being quite a person, altogether.

He was beginning to feel more cheerful now about their prospects. They were descending steadily – and the cautious plod down the glacier, though slow, was still a lot quicker than the passage down the rock face had been. The axe probes had become automatic, the descent had acquired a rhythm...

Suddenly, without any warning, without a hint of weakness from his axe, the ground gave way and Royce was falling in a cloud of flying snow. There was a jerk at his waist that checked but failed to hold him. He was still going down. Then there was another jerk – and he stopped. He was swinging free in semi-darkness, suspended by his waist, still gripping his ice axe.

It took him a moment or two to collect his

wits. Then he parked the axe in his waist loop, groped in his pocket for the free end of the Prusik sling and dropped it down by his left foot. He knew he had to work fast. Already, the pressure of the rope around his chest was making breathing difficult and painful. If he couldn't relieve the constriction he'd be unconscious in a very few minutes – and that would be the end. Only self-help could save him... He fought with the Prusik knot, trying to slide it up a little, trying to get the sling in the right place for his foot. The knot was moving. That was better. He found the sling with his foot, put some weight on it, and got support. Now for the other one. He drew the second knot down and slid his right foot into the sling. He stood up on the slings, jamming both knots tight. At last the pressure was off his chest and he could breathe normally. So far, so good...

He brushed the snow from his face and looked up. He was hanging about twelve feet below the lip. In the dim light he could just make out that the crevasse was bell-shaped, narrow at the top and widening out below – the worst kind to get out of. On all sides, the ice walls were out of reach. There'd be no help from them. He looked down. The bottom of the crevasse, fifteen feet below him, was piled with jagged ice, its tips pointing up like spears...

He could hear Varya's voice, calling. The

voice sounded faint and far away and he couldn't make out what she was saying. She hadn't thrown down the bight of spare rope to help his climb, and he called out to her at the top of his lungs – 'Send the rope!' But nothing happened. Probably she couldn't hear what he said, either. Anyway, he couldn't afford to wait. The crevasse was an ice box and already he felt a numbing cold creeping through him. He'd better get moving, while he could still help himself.

He took a long breath, and started the slow ascent up the ladder of slings. Weight off one foot. Push the Prusik knot a little higher up the climbing rope. Foot back in the sling, jamming the knot. Weight off the other foot. Push the second knot a little higher. Foot back in the second sling... Each time, a few inches gained. Sometimes a few inches lost, when the knot failed to grip on the wet nylon. But keep going! Don't think about the distance still to be covered. Don't think about the belay up above, on which all depends. Don't think about the spears of ice below. Don't think about aching arm muscles and ebbing strength. Just keep going. And remember, you've done it before. You know it works...

Foot by anxious foot, he raised himself. Several times he shouted to Varya that he was all right, that he was climbing. Each time she called back, but with indistinguishable words. She still hadn't sent the bight of rope down – the rope that would have immeasurably eased his ascent. He couldn't understand it. But now he was almost at the top. He looked up as his head touched snow. He saw that the climbing rope had cut deep into the lip of the crevasse and he'd come up under a snow overhang that blocked his path. He'd have to clear it before he could get out. Balancing on the Prusik slings, he took his axe and hacked away at the obstruction, bringing the loose snow down in great lumps on his head and shoulders. Gradually he opened a passage. He raised himself as high as the slings would take him and grasped the top of the climbing rope. This was where a steady pull from above on a separate rope would have helped most – but somehow he'd have to manage without it. He jammed his feet against the snow wall, tightened his grip on the rope, and in one gigantic effort of will and muscle heaved himself out on to the lip.

3

Varya was sitting on the ground twenty feet away, clutching – or so it seemed – the head of the axe she had thrust deep into the snow. As Royce struggled up from the lip, taking the tension off the rope, she unjammed the belay and hugged her right hand to her chest.

Her face was white, and drawn with pain. Around the axe there were traces of blood.

Royce staggered through the snow and dropped down beside her. 'You're hurt! What is it?'

'When you fell,' she said in a faint voice, 'my thumb was caught between the rope and the axe.'

'Let me see.'

She held out her hand. The flesh across the back of her thumb was bruised black and laid open to the bone.

Royce looked at it, and groaned. 'You belayed with it still caught. And all my weight was on it…! Oh, Varya!'

'I had to,' she said. 'There was no time. The rope was slipping – I had to jam it at once.'

Royce nodded. With a crevasse fall, every second counted. By moving fast, at such horrible cost, she'd undoubtedly saved his life.

He took the first-aid kit from his sack and unstoppered a tiny flask of brandy. 'Here – have a mouthful of this.'

Varya put it to her lips, swallowed, spluttered, and passed it back.

Royce examined the hand again, frowning. Then he covered the wound with an antiseptic dressing and bandaged it carefully, so that the fingers were left free. 'How much does it hurt?'

'It is bearable.'

'Would you like some Codeine?'

'Later, perhaps – not now...' The colour was returning to her face and she looked much better. 'I am sorry for my clumsiness.'

'Yes – they'll probably take your badge away!' Royce said.

She didn't smile. 'I could not throw you the bight – I could not help you at all. I was so afraid for you...'

'Well, you can relax,' Royce said. 'It's all over. Just one of those incidents... What we've got to worry about now is the state of your hand.'

'I do not think it will hamper me too much. For climbing, the fingers are more important than the thumb.'

Royce looked at her doubtfully. 'You've had a bad shock. I'm wondering if you ought to go on to-day...'

'Of course we must go on,' she said. Her uninjured hand tightened into a fist. '*Nada vitserapat!*'

'What does that mean?'

'*"Vitserapat"*? It means to tear at something with all your strength – a difficulty – a problem – anything. To tear out success. Never to give in... There are two more hours of daylight. We cannot afford to waste them.'

Royce nodded, knowing she was right. Two hours lost now might mean an extra night on the mountain – perhaps the difference between life and death. 'Very well,' he said. 'But we'll get off the glacier. We can't risk a second crevasse – I doubt if you could belay me with your hand in that condition. Let's work our way to the right and see if we can get back on to the face.'

He slid his two Prusik slings along the rope to their starting points, shouldered his sack, gave Varya an encouraging smile, and set off once more through the cloud.

The few hundred yards they had to cross to reach firm ground were as anxious a passage as any they had made. Royce moved now with an extremity of caution, testing and re-testing, flogging ahead with his axe, stamping down hard on each bit of snow before he committed himself to it. The going was painfully slow, but his care was rewarded. In half an hour they had reached the edge of the glacier and the crevasse danger was behind them. They crossed a narrow fissure by a firm snow bridge, unroped, and tied on again to the long doubled nylon. Then they climbed out of the *couloir* up slopes of easy rock, Royce still leading. A long but straightforward traverse around a contour brought them very soon to the eastern end of the precipitous south face. Varya appeared to be climbing as well as ever in spite of her injury and when she insisted that she could safely take over as pathfinder again, Royce allowed her to go ahead.

They made excellent progress during the

final hour of daylight. Two short pitches with safe holds and good stances brought them to the top of a slanting chimney which in turn took them down nearly a hundred feet without great effort. At the bottom there was a ledge, about four feet deep and thirty long, and with dusk approaching Royce decided it was as good a bivouac spot as they were likely to find. They would have to manage without the tent, but at least there was room to cook a meal, and to sleep.

The face below was sheer, and safety measures were clearly called for. Royce made a quick reconnaissance while the light still held and found good cracks at each end of the ledge. He drove in pitons, fixed snap rings, and linked them with the spare rope from his sack. Then he attached Varya to the rope with a short sling and a free-running ring. 'Just to make sure you don't run away in the night!' he said. He repeated the process for himself. The safety line was slack enough for them to move in comfort along the ledge, to sit or lie down, but tight enough to prevent them stepping over the edge in the dark. Secure on their new rope, they untied from the one they'd climbed with. Royce coiled it, and tied it and the two rucksacks to another piton in the centre of the ledge. All was now set for the night.

'How's the hand?' Royce asked.

Varya was nursing it. 'Now that we have

stopped, it is not very good. I think perhaps I will have that Codeine.'

Royce gave her three tablets, which she swallowed with snow water from her bottle. 'I don't suppose the climbing's improved it,' he said.

'No – but I am glad we came on.'

Royce nodded, and got out the petrol stove. 'We'll both feel better with some food and drink inside us. One way and another it's been quite a day.'

'A day I shall never forget,' Varya said. 'It seems a miracle that you are safe.'

'A miracle?' Royce grinned. 'That's no way for a Marxist to talk!'

He had a little trouble with the petrol stove on the draughty ledge, but by using a corner of the tent fabric as a wind break he managed at last to get it working properly. The final ration of petrol was a short one and he went quickly about the necessary chores before it ran out. First, water for the next day. He collected snow from the ledge and melted it and filled both bottles. Then he put on the pot for the hoosh. As soon as the mixture was steaming, he melted more snow in a billycan and heated water for coffee. As it came to the boil, the stove went out.

They were in near-darkness now. Hopefully, Royce lit a candle and stuck it in a crack in the rock, but it quickly flickered out.

167

He groped in his sack for the small torch he'd brought and put it in the crack instead. 'It won't last long,' he said, 'but it should see us through the meal. Right – let's eat.'

They were both ravenous, and the food was soon gone – all except a few biscuits and a bar of chocolate which Royce said they'd better save for the morning. He divided the last of the sugar for the coffee, and filled his pipe with the last grains of his tobacco.

'Well, it's quite a snug spot here,' he said cheerfully.

Varya smiled. 'I would hardly call it snug. But I have known worse.'

'Is the Codeine beginning to work?'

'Yes, thank you. I feel almost no pain now...' She looked down into the void. 'How far do you think we have still to go?'

Royce shrugged. 'I hope not much more than fifteen hundred feet.'

'Then we have descended half-way.'

'If I'm right.'

Varya sighed. 'It seems like a dream – that I should have climbed down with you, that I should be spending the night on this ledge with you. A long dream ... I can hardly believe that we met only two days ago.'

'It's been an intensive course,' Royce said. 'You'll have quite a tale to tell your boy friend when you get back to Moscow.'

Varya laughed. 'To which boy friend do you refer?'

'The special one, of course,'

'I am afraid there is no special one.'

'How's that?'

'I suppose I have not met him...' She broke off, pointing down the cliff. 'Look – the cloud is lifting. I can see a light. And another...'

Royce gazed down. The cloud was clearing fast. Very soon he could see a whole chain of lights, curving away into the distance. The path of the day's descent had evidently been farther to the east than he'd realised. To-morrow, if conditions remained the same, he and Varya would be visible through glasses to the Russian border watchers. Not that that mattered now...

'Do you know what those lights are?' he asked.

Varya shook her head.

'They're the lights along the Soviet fron-tier fence. They're always on at night, so the guards can make sure that no one climbs over.'

'That is a good thing,' Varya said. 'It is necessary that unwelcome people should be kept out of one's country.'

Royce grinned. 'The fence isn't to keep people out – it's to keep people in! Your fel-low citizens, who would like to leave Russia but aren't allowed to.'

'I do not believe that.'

'You don't? If they were free to choose, there'd be a stampede.'

'You are teasing me. I have never met any such people...' Varya was silent for a while. Then she said, 'You are always talking to me of freedom.'

'It's an important subject.'

'When you use the word, what is in your mind?'

'Many things,' Royce said. 'But first, I suppose, the right to criticise authority without being afraid the secret police will knock on the door in the night.'

'I criticise much in my country. Do you imagine *I* am afraid?'

'I'm sure you're not,' Royce said. 'But then your criticisms are no doubt very minor ones. Like wanting cleaner streets or warmer swimming baths! You don't oppose your government on big issues. Broadly, you conform – so naturally you feel safe.'

'In our country we do not wish to oppose. We know that the government has our interests at heart. Why should we be against it?'

'Some Russians are. Some of your writers, who are in prison at this moment. But perhaps you haven't heard about them?'

'I have heard. I have read about them in the Moscow evening paper. They were disloyal. They wrote bad things about the Soviet Union.'

'They criticised the way the country was being run – that's all.'

'I think they did more. I think they were

enemies of the people, and therefore deserved to be put in prison.'

Royce smiled. 'You would think that, of course.'

'Why do you always smile when we talk of these things? As though you were so wise and I was so stupid.'

'It's better than crying. Or getting angry.'

'You do not take my political views seriously?'

'Not very.'

'Why not?'

'Well, I think you're just repeating what you've been told – and that hardly adds up to a serious view. If you're going to have an opinion that's worth anything you've got to understand and consider all the arguments on the other side. You've also got to have access to the facts. *You* just go along with the dogma. You've never tried to think things out for yourself.'

'Perhaps not,' Varya said. 'Perhaps, in that sense, I am not a political person at all. But I am loyal.'

'To your secret police?'

'To my country… And it is foolish the way you talk always of our secret police, as though they were dreadful men who pounce on innocent victims. I have known many officers in the K.G.B., and they are not at all like that. Several of them are my friends.'

'There are friends and friends,' Royce said.

'I dare say Stalin and Trotsky used to slap each other on the back occasionally – until the crunch came... The thing is, Varya, you're privileged. You said so yourself. You're a Master of Sport. You're almost part of the Establishment. You meet these powerful men socially, as equals. You've never had any occasion to some up against them politically. You've never been ill-treated by them.'

'And I am not likely to be,' Varya said. 'I tell you they are good, honest men, fighting our enemies. They are men I admire and trust.'

Royce gave a tolerant nod. 'Well, let's hope you never have any reason to change your view.'

'What could make me change it?'

'Nothing short of a political earthquake, I should think. Or possibly – falling in love with a man who had a different view.'

'That is ridiculous.'

'I believe it's been known to happen,' Royce said.

Silence fell again. Royce puffed quietly at his pipe. Presently Varya said, 'There is no doubt the weather is changing. I can see two bright stars.'

Royce nodded. 'We'll probably have a very fine day to-morrow.'

'Then we need not have climbed down after all.'

'That's what it looks like – though we couldn't know... Are you sorry?'

172

'To be sorry at this stage would be silly,' Varya said. She untied the knot that held her rucksack and took it from its peg. 'I think it will be cold to-night, now that the cloud is going. Perhaps we should try to get some sleep while we can.'

They put on all their spare clothes and slid into their sleeping sacks. Royce arranged the tent so that it could be pulled over them as an additional covering. Varya turned down the ear flaps of her fur hat and tied the strings under her chin. Royce rolled down his balaclava. Then they stretched out side by side on the bare rock, linked to the safety rope that ran between them.

Sleep didn't come quickly to either of them. The drama of the day had left them tired in body but active in mind. And Varya had been right about the change of temperature. As the sky cleared, an intense frost settled on the ledge. The cold of the rock beneath them penetrated their sacks. Both of them were restless, moving continually, unable to settle down. They dozed fitfully.

Some time during the night, Varya turned on her side towards Royce. Half asleep, he put an arm around her shoulders, the other round her body, and drew her close to him. The cold troubled them less after that.

They were wakened at the same moment by an engine roar that grew steadily louder. Royce shot into a sitting position and rolled back the balaclava from his face. With surprise he saw that it was almost broad daylight. He looked out, blinking in the brightness, trying to spot the helicopter. Yes – there it was! Swooping down from the south-east, coming in now directly opposite the ledge. At first he took it for granted that the machine was the one that had brought him and Brogan to the mountain – but as it flew nearer and began to hover fifty feet away he saw that it was a larger type, and that it had a red star on its fuselage.

'It is Russian!' Varya exclaimed. 'It is one of ours!' She waved excitedly to the uniformed men in the cockpit. One of them waved back – then, with a shrug and hands outstretched in a gesture of impotence, indicated there was nothing they could do to help. The face of the mountain was so nearly vertical that there could be no question of taking the climbers off or even of getting supplies to them. For a few seconds the helicopter continued to hover at a safe distance. Then it banked away and flew off quietly to the north-east.

Royce gazed out from the ledge with a feeling of exhilaration that he hadn't known since the start of the trip. Overnight, a tremendous change had taken place in their surroundings. The day was clear and sparkling, the sky cloudless, the irregularities of the face no longer obscured by mist but sharply etched. Frost particles glistened in the still air. The snow pockets on the mountain side and the snow-covered plain below were a dazzling white. Looking down, Royce thought that his estimate of fifteen hundred feet to the bottom had been about right. A straight plunge – so sheer that if they'd had them they could almost have jumped with parachutes...

He turned to Varya. 'Well, how's the hand this morning?'

'It is rather stiff,' she said. She moved the fingers, painfully. 'And it is throbbing a little.'

She held out the bandaged thumb and Royce examined it. The flesh around the edge of the bandage was red and puffy. It looked bad – and it would probably get worse, Royce thought, before it got better. He took off the bandage, opened up his first-aid kit, put some penicillin ointment on the wound, and covered it with a fresh dressing. 'We must get down quickly,' he said, 'while you can still use it.'

Varya nodded. 'Perhaps it will become less stiff when I start to climb. And now that the weather is fine, the descent should be much easier...' She extricated herself from her

175

sleeping bag and shook out the ice that had been formed by condensation between the bag and its waterproof cover. 'We slept later than we meant to. It is fortunate that the helicopter woke us.'

'Yes,' Royce said, packing up his own bag. 'I suppose you feel happier now that you've been spotted by your fellow countrymen?'

'It is reassuring.'

'They shouldn't have been here, of course. The helicopter was well over the frontier. Typical!'

'You cannot blame them from trespassing when they were searching for me,' Varya said. 'On a humanitarian mission in the mountains, frontiers surely do not matter?'

Royce smiled. 'Well, we won't start the day with an argument.' He got out the few remaining biscuits and the bar of chocolate from his sack and divided them. It was a poor way to begin a long, hard day, but better than nothing.

They finished the scanty repast in a few moments, and drank a little water from their bottles. Then, as the first yellow rays of the sun showed above the horizon, they prepared to leave. Their boots had frozen stiff during the night and they had to knead them before they were soft enough to force their feet inside. Royce packed the rucksacks, coiled with some difficulty the ice-encrusted safety line, and retrieved all but one of the pitons. In ten minutes they were roped and ready to go.

'Okay,' Royce said, as he anchored himself to the remaining piton. 'Over the side with you!'

During the first hour or two they made excellent progress. The part of the face they were descending, though sensationally steep, was more broken than the one they had tackled the previous morning, and it offered good holds and convenient stances not too far apart. There was still no question of being able to prospect a route all the way to the ground, since rock obstructions blocked the view, but at least they could see far enough below them to be able to make sure of the next pitch. Whenever possible they roped down, saving both time and effort. The only exceptional hazards were the occasional boulders and stones that came hurtling down from above as the rapidly rising temperature thawed the ice. But neither of the climbers suffered any injury – and after the long days and nights of cloud they were glad to feel the warm southern sun on their backs. They were heartened, too, in mid-morning, by the arrival of a second helicopter. This time, it *was* the Turkish one. The crew men were the same as before, and the security officer, Enver, was again aboard. The machine hovered close by for a moment or two, the crew men waving encouragingly,

Enver waving and staring. Then it sank down to the foot of the face and landed there to await the climbers' arrival. Royce and Varya resumed the descent.

Cheered by the encounter and hoping to end the climb-down quickly, they managed for a time to keep up their pace – but the effort was taxing and by noon they were both beginning to flag. They had been on the move almost continuously for more than five hours, in exposed conditions involving the greatest mental and physical stress, and not even a sweet or a lump of sugar to sustain them and no prospect of food before the evening. Though Varya didn't complain, the strained look on her face showed that her hand was hurting badly, and more tablets of painkiller seemed to make little difference. For her, the climb down had become an ordeal. Royce, trying not to think of the seven or eight hundred precipitous feet still to be mastered, belayed and watched her with increasing care. For a while their descent, though slower, remained steady. Then, around two o'clock, their advance was abruptly checked.

Varya had just pioneered a long and awkward pitch to a roomy stance, and Royce had joined her there. Ahead of them there was a slot in the mountain, a bottomless gully twenty feet wide. On the side where they were standing there were neither holds nor stances, except for the one they occupied. A descent of the flank was impossible. The rock face above the gully was an overhung slab, cut by a fissure some twelve feet along its length, but otherwise almost smooth. Just above the level where the face turned under, the running right across to the far flank, there was a narrow ledge of a different rock – an obtruding shaly stratum, no more than six inches wide.

In silence, Royce studied the ledge. The traverse was one of the least attractive he had ever seen. The rock was weathered, flaking and visibly unsound. In places it was less than a couple of inches thick – a mere wafer. As a way across it was even less appealing than the ice slope he'd traversed with Brogan on the ascent – for here there was no saving slope where a slip could be arrested. The exposure was total. A fall might well result in a snapped rope – and a snapped rope would mean certain death on the plain six hundred feet below.

Yet beyond the ledge there was the promise of a safe and rapid descent. The far flank of the gully, unlike the nearer one, was well broken and not unduly steep. Royce could see an excellent stance and anchoring point, and a good crack leading down from it for several hundred feet. If they could make the traverse, they might well be off the mountain in three hours and all their troubles would be over.

The alternative was the too familiar one – to climb back the way they'd come and seek a new route. Through his glasses Royce scrutinised the towering slab of rock above them. Apart from their path of descent, there was no hint of a break in its surface. They might have to retrace their steps for hours before they found a way round and down again. They would certainly have to spend a second night on the mountain – without food, without water, and with Varya's hand getting steadily worse. By morning she might well be incapable of climbing at all. Then they would be stuck there, unable to move. The chances of any competent expedition being mounted in time to rescue them were negligible.

Royce looked at Varya. Her face, grey and drawn, moved him to pity. He had never felt more responsible, more desperately anxious to make the right decision – or less certain what decision to make. It was the kind of situation that had confronted him more than once since the start of the trip – but never had the danger been so acute, or the prize so great.

'Well,' he said, 'I'm afraid it's a choice of evils. What do you think?'

Varya looked up at the slab – and then across the gully. 'I think we must take the risk.'

Royce nodded, and turned towards the ledge.

He stepped out delicately, facing the rock, pressing himself against it to get the maximum friction support, seeking with sensitive fingers for the tiniest irregularities in the surface. Inch by inch, he edged his way along. Once, something gave way under his right foot and he saved himself only by transferring his weight immediately to his left. He could feel the sweat pouring down inside his clothes. He glanced ahead to the fissure. Six feet – five feet... At least that would give him a respite, if he could reach it. A few more steps. Three feet – two feet. Almost there... He stretched out with his left hand, and found a hold at last, and drew himself into the rock haven. He'd made it...

The fissure was wider and a lot deeper than he'd thought. It had a platform that was roomy enough for him to stand on in comfort, roomy enough to take two of them at a pinch. An adequate stance, with a good rock knob for an anchorage. He paused for a while, considering how best to secure Varya when she moved, considering his options.

If he continued to the far flank, he would be well placed to help her if she came off – but with a twenty-foot run-out, a fall might swing her against the flank with crippling force. A terrible risk... He could fix a run-

ning belay at the fissure before he went on –
but the serrations of the ledge might jam the
nylon and turn the belay into a direct one,
with the chance of a snapped rope... Or he
could stay where he was, anchored, ready to
check a fall with the resilience of his body,
and wait for Varya to join him. If all went
well, and she reached him, they'd be more
than half-way home. But if she fell, she'd be
dangling in space below him. How would he
get her up...? He looked ahead at the eight
feet of ledge still to be crossed. Only eight
feet. Crazy, of course – but there'd be risks
whatever he did...

He made himself fast to the knob of rock
and called out 'On belay!' Varya stepped on
to the ledge, pale but unhesitating. She, too,
pressed herself close to the face, seeking the
minute finger holds he'd used, carefully
avoiding the bit of ledge that had crumbled
under his foot. Royce took in the slack of the
rope over his shoulder, leaning back, watching her every move. Nothing in his own transit had given him a fraction of the anxiety he
felt now. Seven feet to go – six feet... Suddenly there was a crack and the ledge
collapsed under her. She was falling. Royce
braced himself, taking the mighty tug around
his back, taking all the weight he could for
the vital first seconds. Then the rope ran out,
tightened on his waist snap ring, pulled him
outwards. But the anchor held. And the rope

hadn't broken. There was still hope.

He looked down. Varya was swinging in the void, twelve feet below him. On her face there was an expression almost of despair. She called out something, in a strangled voice. Already, the pressure of the rope was constricting her. In minutes, it would be too late to help her.

Royce gripped his waist loop with both hands, contracted his stomach muscles, and swivelled his body round inside the loop till he was facing the rock. With the free end of the climbing rope he made a bight and threw it over the anchor knob and secured it to the snap ring at his waist. Then he untied the knot of his waist loop, and freed himself, and stepped away, leaving Varya hanging directly from the anchorage.

Unroped and unsupported, he stepped out on to the last eight feet of the ledge. He covered the distance in three quick strides, almost at a run, angled out over the chasm and relying on speed to make up for lack of balance. As he reached for the safety of firm rock, the ledge broke beneath him. He hurled himself forward, hands outstretched, scrabbling at the gully wall. His left hand found a projection as his feet dropped. For a moment he hung by his hand. Then his scraping boots found a lodgment and he heaved himself up.

The stance he had marked down from the other side was six feet below him. In seconds he had reached it. He took his spare rope from his sack and quickly anchored. Then he tied a loop in the free end of the rope and called to Varya 'Catch hold!' He threw the rope three times before she caught it. In her physical distress she could do no more than slip an arm through the loop and hold on – but that was enough. Royce hauled on the rope, drawing her in to the flank in an upward arc. As her feet touched rock he leaned over, linking his fingers in hers, letting the anchor rope take the strain. Then, with a great heave, he hoisted her to safety.

'Oh, *Varya!*' he said, and took her in his arms.

There were no more problems, no more setbacks. Though they'd lost their long rope, they had enough spares to take them to the bottom. The crack below the stance offered all they needed in the way of holds and they descended its three hundred feet in less than half an hour. An easy diagonal traverse took them to a short chimney, and below the chimney the face was still well broken. They roped down the last hundred feet of the mountain in two quick stages, reaching the foot as dusk was falling. They put on crampons and clawed their way down the last snow slope to the waiting helicopter. As they staggered up to it, Enver stepped out to meet them.

CHAPTER IV

THE AFTERMATH

The Turk had come well-prepared to succour the two tired and hungry climbers. As they struggled out of their packs and dropped into the helicopter seats he produced flasks of hot coffee, and cheese and bread, which they fell upon avidly. Not until they were feeling a bit restored did he start to ask questions – and then he confined himself to the basic ones.

'Where is Captain Brogan, Mr Royce?'

'He's dead,' Royce said.

Enver inclined his head. 'I feared that must be so, when I saw he was not with you on the mountain… And what of his mission?'

'He succeeded in destroying the camera,' Royce said. 'But at the cost of his life.'

'I am sorry… What caused this tragedy?'

'Well…' Royce began – and paused. He had caught a warning glance from Varya, and remembered in time that he'd promised to be discreet in his statements until she was safely out of the country. Vagueness seemed the best bet – with no mention of frontiers. 'He was swept away, Mr Enver, by a fall of snow and ice set off by the explosion. It overtook him before he had time to get clear.'

Enver nodded slowly. 'A most regrettable loss... And how did you come to meet this young lady?'

'She was one of a party of Russians who were climbing up from the other side,' Royce said. 'Her name is Varya Lermontov, and she speaks English... Varya, this is Mr Enver. He is – he made all the arrangements for Captain Brogan and myself.'

Enver gave Varya a look. 'You are seeking refuge in our country, Miss Lermontov?'

'Indeed I am not,' Varya said indignantly. 'Why should I wish for refuge?'

Royce hastened to explain. 'The two male climbers of Miss Lermontov's party were also involved in a fatality, Mr Enver. The mountain was in a very dangerous state – and they were carried away by another fall of snow. Miss Lermontov and I met on the summit after the accident. As the only survivors, we were dependent on each other for our safe descent. A rope was essential, you understand. It was a question of which side of the mountain we climbed down – and Miss Lermontov agreed to descend with me. That's the only reason she's here – and she'd like to return to Russia as soon as possible.'

'I see. In that case, we must try to arrange it...' He paused. 'So you'd no trouble with the Russian expedition, Mr Royce?'

'None at all. We had no encounter or

communication with them at any time.'

'That is very satisfactory,' Enver said.

There was no bath at the guest house, but the servant Ahmet had prepared an abundant supply of hot water, which served almost as well. Varya bathed her hand, and Royce put more penicillin and a new dressing on it, and re-bandaged it. The cut had been inflamed further by the day's climbing, but they agreed that a few extra hours without proper attention would probably do it no harm. Presently they joined Enver in the big room downstairs for the first real meal either of them had had for many days. Once more Ahmet had produced a feast, with tender lamb chops and a delicious dish of aubergines, cucumbers and tomatoes. As they ate, Royce described some of their adventures on the mountain – particularly his fall into the crevasse when, as he emphasised, Varya's tenacity and endurance had saved his life. Varya, her eyes heavy with fatigue, said little.

They drank coffee and smoked a cigarette. Enver said: 'You are, I can see, in great need of sleep, and though I am interested in all you tell me I must not keep you up. To-morrow we will talk again... There will, of course, be a few questions I must put to Miss Lermontov – but they can wait until the morning.'

Varya looked up sharply. 'I am to be interrogated?'

187

'A mere formality, I assure you.'

'I've heard of these formalities. First come the questions and then the arrest.'

'Arrest...?' Enver looked at her in surprise. 'For what, may I ask?'

'I am here in your country without permission, without papers.'

He smiled. 'You are here in very exceptional circumstances, Miss Lermontov. It is like the emergency landing of an aeroplane, or a shipwreck – one does not expect papers. In any case, as a friend of Mr Royce and one who has done so much to make his safe return possible, you are more than welcome. In this respect I am sure I can speak for the authorities. I shall require from you only those useless particulars which in all countries have to be written down on forms when people cross frontiers – your full name, your parents' names, your place of birth and so on... Then you will be free to leave for Russia as soon as it can be arranged.'

'You promise that?'

'I think it most unlikely that there will be any difficulty.'

Varya still looked doubtful. Royce gave her uninjured hand a soothing pat. 'Relax,' he said. 'You've nothing at all to worry about...' He turned to Enver. 'What are the plans for to-morrow?'

'If the weather remains good,' Enver said, 'there will be an aeroplane here at nine

188

o'clock in the morning to fly us to Ankara. I took the liberty of dispatching a radio message to your embassy when you were first observed descending the mountain, and Sir John Avery is expecting you. To-night I will also send word of the death of Captain Brogan, so that you will be spared the necessity of breaking this sad news.'

Royce nodded. 'I'd appreciate that.'

'In the meantime,' Enver said, 'I am afraid there is a little problem that we face. Unfortunately we have only one guest room here and only two comfortable beds. I do not know what arrangements you wish to make. I was not, of course, expecting a lady guest... Perhaps we might dismantle one of the beds and bring it down here?'

Varya gave a weary smile. 'Mr Royce and I have spent a night in a tent together, and a night on a mountain ledge. I think we can share a room without impropriety.'

Enver bowed gravely. 'In that case, I will wish you both a sound night's sleep.'

They were wakened in the morning by Ahmet, who arrived just before eight with the usual breakfast of tea, cheese, butter and unleavened bread. They had slept without stirring for nearly ten hours and they both felt completely refreshed. Varya's hand had given her no trouble and Royce decided to leave the bandage alone till they got to

189

Ankara. He sluiced his face in cold water and went for a brisk walk round the edge of the airfield, enjoying the frosty sunshine and the feel of level ground under his feet again. By the time he returned, Enver had taken the particulars he required from a still-suspicious Varya, and the plane was waiting.

They reached Ankara without incident after a smooth, two-hour flight. An official car, ordered by Enver, was waiting at the airport to take them on. The Turk showed them in and then stood by the door, smiling, and holding out his hand. 'This is where I leave you,' he said. 'I shall, of course, continue to keep in touch with your movements, and I shall be available if you need any help – but I am sure that your respective embassies will be able to do all for you that is now necessary. Good-bye, Mr Royce – it has been a great honour and pleasure to meet you. Good-bye, Miss Lermontov – and have a good flight to Moscow.' He stood back and waved as the car drew away.

Royce pushed back the glass panel of the limousine and spoke to the driver. 'You know where to go, do you? – the British Embassy.' The man half turned, and nodded.

Varya said quickly, 'That is for you, but not for me. Will you please ask him to set me down at my own embassy?'

Royce looked at her. 'What – *now?*'

'That is where I must go,' Varya said.

'I know – but not this minute, surely…? You'll be expected to give a full account of everything as soon as you're there – why rush into a lot of tiring explanations before you've had time to draw breath? They'll probably want to whisk you off to Russia straight away, too. I know you're anxious to get back, but – well, I did hope to see a bit more of you before you left.'

'I think I should go now,' Varya said, in a flat voice. 'I would like it if you would give the instruction.'

Royce fought down a growing sense of panic. 'I don't understand why you're in such a hurry. You've only just got here. Surely you can give yourself a few hours… After all, if the weather hadn't been as kind as it was this morning, you could easily be spending another day in Kars.'

'But I am not in Kars,' Varya said. 'And I shall not feel entirely comfortable in my mind until I am with my own people again.'

'You're not still afraid of the Turkish secret police, are you?'

'Not, perhaps, as much as I was…'

'Then why won't you feel comfortable?'

'In the sort of situation in which I am,' Varya said, 'it is customary for a Russian to go at once to his embassy.'

'You mean there's some rule about it, some instruction? Report within two hours,

191

or else...?'

'Of course there is no such instruction. Nevertheless, it would be expected. And for a Soviet citizen it is the natural thing to do.'

Royce looked at her ironically. 'The way it's natural for a homing pigeon to make for the loft?'

'The loft? What is that?'

'The place where the pigeon's trainer keeps it.'

'Ah... Now I think you are trying to start another argument.'

'No,' Royce said. 'I'm simply trying to get at your reason for wanting to hurry... Tell me, would anything unpleasant happen to you if you went to your embassy to-morrow instead of to-day?'

'Unpleasant...? Of course not.'

'You feel free to make your own choice?'

'Well – yes...'

'Would you find one more day with me unbearable?'

'You know that is a foolish question.'

'Then may I suggest a programme for the next twenty-four hours that I think would please you?'

Varya sat silent for a moment. Then she said, 'What is your programme?'

'Come with me to my embassy. Let me introduce you to the people I know there – they'll be proud and delighted to meet you and I know they'll make you very welcome for the night. Let me tell them about your climbing and show you off a little. Have your hand properly attended to. Then see something of the town. You may never be able to leave Russia again, you know – this could be your one opportunity to learn something of how the outside world lives. You wouldn't want to miss that opportunity, surely… And this evening let me take you out to diner – somewhere gay and exciting, with music and dancing – and we'll celebrate our safe descent of the mountain… Doesn't that programme appeal to you?'

'It appeals very much,' Varya said. 'But…' She hesitated. 'How can I go to your embassy, and to dinner with you, looking like this?'

'That's no problem – they'll fit you out with something… Please, Varya! There are things I want to talk to you about before you go. Important things. If I've got to say good-bye to you, I'd like to do it in a civilized way. Surely you don't want us to part on a street corner, after all we've been through together?'

Varya looked away from him, out of the window. 'I think it would be a mistake,' she said. 'I think it is better that I go now.'

'Without my letter of commendation? "You are a wonderful climber, Varya." Signed "William Royce"?'

She smiled. 'Now you are being absurd.'

Royce put his hand over hers on the car seat. 'Just one day! Is it such an unreasonable request for a man to make?'

She sat without speaking. The car sped on. Royce waited. He could feel his heart hammering. Yes, or no...? It was worse than crossing a crumbling ledge...

'Very well,' she said at last. 'I too would prefer to say good-bye in a civilized way.... Since you wish it, I will stay with you until to-morrow.'

2

Their welcome at the British Embassy was as warm and friendly as Royce had known it would be. The ambassador was relieved to have Royce safely back, quietly congratulatory over the outcome of his mission, and highly intrigued by the girl he'd brought down the mountain with him. Lady Avery, a handsome, lively woman in her late forties, was delighted to meet Royce at last, and no less intrigued by his companion. After he had explained the situation, she not only asked, but insisted, that Varya should remain as her guest for as long as she wished – and meanwhile promised to take good care of her until Royce collected her for dinner. In no time at all she had carried her off to some remote part of the building, talking rapidly of baths, clothes and hair-do's.

Royce spent an hour alone with the ambassador, giving him a faithful account of all that had happened on the mountain – but mentioning at the end his personal undertaking to Varya and the reason for it. Avery, once he'd learned that the girl would probably be leaving Turkey within a day or two, saw no problem. The Turks and the Americans, he said, would obviously wish for a report on the mission, and it would have to be a full and accurate one – particularly as the girl would be certain to give her own full account to the Russians when she got back. But nobody would expect a man who had just returned from an very gruelling expedition to sit down at once and write out a statement about it. A pause for recuperation was in order. If Royce would let him have something on paper before he left for India, Avery would see that it was held back until the girl was safely on her way home – though he agreed with Royce that her fears were quite groundless.

Before he left the embassy, Royce looked in on Tommy Garson and had a friendly word with him. He told him, in brief outline, what he'd told the ambassador, and mentioned the Russian girl who'd climbed down with him.

Garson was as interested as the others had been. 'What's she like? – short, bulging and dedicated, I suppose.'

'She's not particularly short,' Royce said. 'She's certainly a serious young woman … I want to take her out to dinner to-night and show her a bit of life. Any suggestions where we might go?'

'What sort of place are you thinking of?' Garson asked.

'Oh, somewhere bright and cheerful, where we can dance. Not too dressy.'

'Turkish food?'

'I really don't mind, as long as it's good.'

'Well, I'd try Fawzi's, if I were you – about half a mile along the Boulevard on the left. There are green lamps outside – you can't miss it. But you'd better give them a tinkle and reserve a table – they tend to fill up.'

'I'll do that,' Royce said. 'Thanks a lot.'

He collected the van, which he'd left garaged behind the embassy, and drove to the Kara Palace Hotel, thankful that he'd retained his room. He bathed, and shaved the week's stubble from his face, and put on a dark suit for the evening. Then he sat down and wrote a letter to the American general, Burns, c/o the American Embassy, telling him without going into details that after a brilliant climb Captain Brogan had sacrificed his life in carrying out the task entrusted to him; and expressing his own deep regret at the loss of a fine companion. A full account of the incident, he said, would be following shortly.

As he finished the letter, his telephone rang. To his surprise, it was Bob Everett on the line – the man who was going to drive with him to India.

'Well, hallo!' Royce said. 'Nice to hear your voice, Bob. Where are you speaking from?'

'The Park Hotel, Istanbul,' Everett told him. 'I got in a day earlier than I expected, so I thought I'd stop off and take a look round. How are things with you?'

'Fine...'

'I hope you haven't been too bored, kicking your heels in Ankara.'

Royce grimaced into the telephone. 'No – I've found the odd thing to do...'

'Good! How are the arrangements? Are we all set?'

'I think so. When are you planning to get here?'

'Around six to-morrow evening.'

'Then we should be able to leave first thing the next morning – on present form, anyway...' Royce paused. 'Look, Bob, now you're on the phone there is one matter I'd like to consult you about.'

'What's that?'

'Well, it's quite hypothetical,' Royce said. 'What you might call contingency planning. The position is this...'

At six-thirty that evening Royce looked in at the Kara Palace's flower shop and bought a single red rose. Then, in a mood that was distinctly short of hopeful, he drove off in the van to keep his dinner date.

In the embassy lobby, he ran into Garson again. 'Hallo,' he said. 'Have you seen Varya?'

Garson grinned. 'Seen her? – I'll say I have! You were holding out on me, old boy – she's terrific! I bet you loitered on your way down the mountain.'

'Don't be an ass... I mean have you seen her around just now?'

'Not for half an hour – probably dressing...' Garson looked quizzically at Royce. 'Are you feeling all right, Bill? You don't look as though you're going to take a gorgeous girl to dinner. You look as though you're about to tackle an impregnable north face.'

'I think I may be,' Royce said.

There was a light step on the stair and Varya appeared. Garson said, 'Well, have a good time, old boy,' and slipped away.

Royce gazed at Varya, not quite believing what he saw. She was wearing a black lace dress with a close-fitting bodice and a deep V neck, revealing a figure that he hadn't even suspected. Her jet black hair fell shining to her shoulders. The lovely curves of her mouth were enhanced by lipstick, sparingly used. She was, he realised with something of a shock, a truly beautiful woman.

'Why are you staring at me?' she asked.

'I'm sorry. It's such a transformation... I had no idea you were that shape.'

'Is it so unusual?'

'I'd got accustomed to breeches, three pullovers and a padded jacket.'

She smiled. 'You look rather different yourself, now that you are clean and without a beard... Where are we going?'

'Just down the road,' Royce said. He took the coat she was carrying and helped her into it. It was of black Persian lamb, with wide sleeves and a dramatic swing at the back. He watched her while she draped her head with a turquoise chiffon scarf. Then, in a kind of trance, he took her arm and steered her out to the van. 'I hope you don't mind the old jalopy – it seemed less stuffy than a hired car. Rope and ironmongery all around – sort of fitting.'

'I like it very much,' Varya said.

As she settled herself in the seat, he gave her the rose. 'For successfully completing your climb! I'll raise the three cheers when we get to the drinks.'

She held it for a moment, delicately sniffing its scent. 'It is beautiful,' she said, and pinned it into the V of her dress. 'Thank you.'

There was a good deal of traffic in the Boulevard and Royce drove slowly. 'I'm sorry I had to leave you for so long,' he said. 'How have you been getting on?'

'I have had a wonderful day. Everyone has been so kind to me.'

'No bright lights shining in your face? No beatings up?'

'Not one. It seems that I was wrong.'

'Did you get your hand fixed?'

'Yes. Lady Avery's doctor called and put some stitches in it, and gave me an injection. Now I shall forget it.'

'Who lent you the clothes?'

'They belong to Lady Avery. I tried on some things of her daughter, but she is not the same size as me – she is too slim.'

'You look marvellous, anyway.'

'Thank you... Lady Avery has been very kind to me – and she has wonderful clothes!'

'Did you manage to see anything of the town?'

'A little. I looked at the shops with Jane, after I had had my hair done. Jane is Lady Avery's daughter. She paid for my hair. She said it was a present, and I accepted gratefully because I have no money... Now I feel a little guilty about everything.'

'Why?'

'I think,' Varya said, 'because I have enjoyed myself so much.'

As a setting for a light-hearted and intimate evening, Fawzi's turned out to be all that Royce could have wished. Its atmosphere was exotic, its décor opulent, its oval bays round the rectangle of dance floor discreetly set apart. It was full enough to be lively without appearing to be crowded. The orchestra was enthusiastic but not deafening. The waiters, in costumes that looked like something out of Haroun Al Raschid, were numerous and attentive. If the evening ended in a bleak non-future, Royce thought, it wouldn't be the fault of Mr Fawzi.

He smiled across the table at Varya. 'What would you like to drink?' he asked. 'Vodka?'

She gave an exaggerated shudder, her shapely shoulders gleaming. 'Vodka is much too strong for me.'

'Well, shall we have champagne right through?'

'If it is to be a celebration, I think so. Also, I like champagne.'

'Good...' Royce ordered a bottle of Pol Riger, and sat back. 'You know, Varya, you look like a million roubles!'

'I am glad you approve of me.'

'Would you care to dance?'

'I would love to.'

Royce led her out on to the floor. The band was playing a slow foxtrot. He took her fingers carefully in his left hand, avoiding the bandaged thumb, and steered her in among the couples. He wasn't surprised to find that she danced beautifully. Most good climbers were good dancers. Except for the fact that she held herself rather far away from him, she was the perfect partner. He remembered what she'd said on that first day's descent of the mountain – that they moved with the same rhythm, they were in harmony. It was as true on the dance floor as it had been on rock. If only it had been true about everything...!

He applied a little pressure and drew her nearer. 'What are you afraid of?' he said teasingly. 'The capitalist embrace?'

She smiled up at him. 'I think it is the Royce embrace I am afraid of!' But after that, she stayed close.

They danced till the champagne'd cooled. Then Royce took her back to the table.

'Well,' he said, as the wine was poured, 'I'd like to propose a toast... To the girl I met on top of a mountain, and to three of the most memorable days of my life!'

Varya raised her glass. 'If I may substitute "the man" for "the girl," I will happily drink to that too... *Do kontza!*'

'What does that mean?'

'I think you call it "bottoms up"!'

Royce laughed. 'Not with champagne, surely – we'll choke.' But he drained his glass, and so did she. 'Right,' he said. 'Now let's see if we can find our way through the menu.'

They chose watermelon, and a dish called *deunerkebab*, which was slices of lamb roasted before them over a charcoal fire by one of the Haroun Al Raschids. Between courses they danced – and when they weren't dancing they chatted lightly, avoiding all serious topics. They ordered more wine and drank more toasts. Over coffee they watched an exuberant floor show, high-lighted by a troupe of whirling dervishes in white jackets and skirts and tall red fezzes...

Then, in spite of the champagne and the cheerful surroundings, preoccupied silences began to occur – and Royce knew that the gay pretence was over. Presently he suggested that they should leave and drive out somewhere for an hour. Varya looked doubtful – but Royce took charge and had her in the van before she could bring herself to a positive 'No.' He drove quickly out to the old city, to a place he remembered, and parked in the darkness and silence of the ancient ruins.

'Now we can talk,' he said.

Varya sat motionless, far away at her end of the seat. 'What is it you wish to say?'

Royce took a deep breath, and plunged. 'It's six days since I was here last. Only six days... but in that time my life's been transformed – because I met you, Varya. And I believe yours has, too. We've come to know each other so well. We've learned to trust each other and rely on each other. We've fought our way down a mountain together. We've staked our lives for each other. We're bound up together. I don't believe we can do without each other now – and be happy. At least, I know I can't do without you... Varya,

203

I'm terribly in love with you. I can't bear the thought that I may never see you again.'

He waited. The silence was so intense that he could here his watch ticking on his wrist.

She gave a little sigh. 'I am honoured that you should feel like that towards me,' she said. 'I admire you very much – more than any man I have known. I have liked being with you. I shall be very sad when we part... But to dwell on these things is useless. I should have gone to my embassy yesterday. I knew that it was a mistake to delay.'

'It wasn't a mistake, Varya – it was right. You didn't go because in your heart you didn't want to. Because you're in love with me, too. Isn't that so?'

'I am in love with you, yes. It is not a thing I can deny when all the time my eyes and actions speak the truth. I am deeply in love with you...'

'Then stay with me, Varya. Marry me. Don't go back to Russia. Come to India and climb with me. Travel with me. There are mountains all over the world that we can explore together. Places I'm longing to show you. Wonderful things we can do together... Oh, darling, say you will.'

'It is impossible,' Varya said. 'You must know it is impossible... Never could I become a defector.'

'A defector? Who said anything about defecting? I'm not suggesting you should change any of your views. I'm not asking you to do any thing or say anything against your country – I know you never would. I'd expect you to be its ambassadress... All I'm asking is that you should marry me and live with me. It's not an unusual thing to happen. All over the world, women leave their own countries to marry foreigners. No one looks upon them as defectors.'

'With us it is different,' Varya said. 'In Russia I would be considered a defector. What is worse, I would feel myself to be one. I could never be happy, knowing that I had deserted – knowing that I had not even made my report on the task which was given to me. I would lose all self-respect.'

'But the task's over,' Royce said. 'It's all in the past now – finished with. Reporting on it can't make any difference.'

'Perhaps not – but I have the obligation... And there are many other things. In Moscow I have duties, responsibilities which I have accepted. I am trusted there – even honoured. I cannot abandon the people I have worked with, the things I believe in, the country I am proud of and which is proud of me – to marry an enemy.'

'You know you don't think of me as an enemy,' Royce said.

'I know I prefer to think of you as a man. But all the same, you *are* an enemy. A political enemy. It is only because you were an enemy that we met on the mountain. And you will not change... How could there be happiness in a marriage where, in so many important ways, there was no agreement, no sympathy? We would always be divided, as the world is divided.'

'The world's a big, complicated place,' Royce said, 'and it doesn't stand still. We can't rule our private lives by what's happening in it at any particular tine. We're two ordinary human beings who belong to each other – that's the most important thing for us. Do personal feelings count with you for so little?'

'They count very much with me, especially at this moment. Do not imagine that it is easy for me to sit and talk like this, instead of falling into your arms, as I long to do.'

'Oh, Varya, if only you would! You seem so far away. Why do we torture ourselves? Darling, surely nothing matters as much as a human relationship – as loving and being loved? To renounce love for some sterile theory – it's a mutilation of life. A crime against nature.'

'Where loyalty is concerned,' Varya said, 'personal feelings must often be set aside. I think you know this, too. You say that love is all, but you do not believe it. Let me ask you a question... If you had not offended against the laws of my country, and if my government were willing to receive you, would you come and live in the Soviet Union for the rest of your life, because you are in love with me and wish to marry me?'

'I would live almost anywhere else with you,' Royce said.

'But you would not come to Russia?'

'No...'

'And I would not expect you to. You have your loyalties, as I have mine. You believe in what you call your free society. You cannot bear the thought of living in a communist country, of giving allegiance to a communist government – even with me. For you, that would be the greatest mutilation.'

'Yes,' Royce said, 'I think it would.'

'So – we have reached the truth. The gulf that separates us is not between loyalty and love, but between different loyalties. What you are asking is that I should give up mine, and embrace yours. But that is not possible, so we must part – even though to-night it tears us in pieces.'

Royce looked out into the darkness. If there was an answer, it escaped him. They had reached the final deadlock – as all along he had feared they would. This was the end of their short road together...

He found Varya's hand and covered it, gently, with his own. It was a gesture of acceptance, of resignation. 'When will you go to your embassy?' he asked.

'I thought at ten to-morrow morning.'

'I would like to say good-bye to you before you leave.'

'I would like that, too.'

'Then I will come just before ten.'

There was a long silence – so long that it seemed as though neither of them would ever break it. It was Varya who spoke at last. 'What are you thinking?'

Sadly, Royce said, 'I'm thinking of the people who have tried to leave your country and not been able to. The people who have been shot down on your frontier wire, trying to escape. The people who've been drowned in seas and blown up on minefields. The people who learned... And then of you, so blindly stubborn, so trusting in all you've been told, so naïve – *free,* by a chance that'll never come again, but determined to go back – to a tyranny, a world of deceit and lies and terror ... I only hope that if the scales ever do fall from your eyes, it won't be too late.'

He pressed the starter and turned the car back on the road.

Royce lay awake for hours that night, frustrated, self-questioning, thinking back over what had been said – wondering if he could have done better, wondering if he'd been too ready to admit defeat, wondering if his approach had been wrong. Perhaps he had talked too much – and allowed Varya to talk too much. Perhaps he should have taken her in his arms, and kissed her, and made love to her, as he'd so much wanted to do. In a torrent of passion, her resistance might have been swept away...

Yet would it really have worked? With many women, yes – but with Varya? Royce doubted it. She might've faltered for a moment – but afterwards? Intelligence and principle and resolution would surely have taken over at the end. Her decision had been largely of the mind. And in the area where it mattered, he hadn't been able to reach her mind at all...

If only he'd had more time! That was the crux of the problem. Time to marshal arguments, to thrash out differences, to get down to the roots of things – above all, to open windows of knowledge which for her had always been kept closed. Given enough time, he might have persuaded her, he might at last have won her mind as well as her heart... But he'd had no time. Three days, to undo the teaching of twenty years. Three days to produce a revelation to work a miracle. No... With a woman like Varya it had been in impossible task from the start...

All the same, when Royce drove to the British Embassy next morning he hadn't finally given up hope. Love could sometimes work its own miracles. Varya, too, might have spent the night in sleepless self-questioning... It was only when he saw her that he knew he must reconcile himself to losing her. She was in the lobby, saying good-bye to Lady Avery and Jane. She was back in her quilted clothes, her rucksack and ice axe over her shoulders. Royce stood by with pretended nonchalance, forcing his features into a social smile, feeling that he was dying inch by inch.

At last it was over. The words of thanks, the good wishes, the final waves. Varya turned to the door. Royce went out with her, and they walked slowly together down the drive.

'So you didn't change your mind,' he said.

'No...'

'Is there anything I can do? Would you like me to run you over to your embassy?'

'No, thank you. I have found out where it is – and I would like to walk.'

Royce nodded. 'Well – this is it, then...' He took her hands in his. 'All I can say is that it's been wonderful knowing you, Varya – even for three days. I hope you have a safe flight to Moscow. Good-bye – and good luck!'

'Good-bye!' she said. She reached up, and put her arms round his neck, and kissed him. For a moment she clung to him. 'Good-bye, William Royce... As long as I live I shall never forget you.'

She turned away, her eyes brimming. Royce stood by the gate and watched her set off along the road. She looked back once, and waved. Then she rounded a corner, and was gone.

3

Varya walked slowly along the pavement, looking in front of her but seeing little, her mind wholly preoccupied with thoughts of Royce and the sorrow of their parting. She hadn't a doubt that she had done what was necessary and right, but she had never in her life felt so unhappy, so utterly empty...

It wasn't until she had gone some distance that she realised she had taken the wrong turning. She was in a quiet back street of small houses, not embassies. Over the top of the buildings she could see the high tower of the Kara Palace Hotel, which was well beyond her destination. She had better make for the Boulevard, she decided, and get fresh directions.

She stopped for a moment to hitch up her rucksack. As she tugged at the strap, a large black limousine drew up beside her at the kerb. Two men jumped out, grabbed hold of her, and bundled her into the back. The door slammed and the car drove on.

For a few seconds she sat motionless between them, almost paralysed with shock and fear. She had no need to ask who they were. Only the Turkish security police would have dared to act like that. What she had been afraid of all along had happened.

Now that she was no longer under William Royce's protection, they were going to interrogate her. Well – from the start she would protest. 'Where are you taking me?' she demanded in Turkish. She got no response. Both men gazed stolidly ahead.

Before she could say anything more the car slid to a halt. It had stopped beside a wrought-iron gate in an unfrequented road. One of the men hauled her out, pushed her through the gate, and hustled her up a garden path to the back entrance of an imposing white building. He went in ahead of her and led the way through a maze of corridors into a large, carpeted lobby. A telephone was ringing in a box near the front door and a man who looked like a porter answered it. 'Soviet Embassy,' he said in Russian.

Varya stared at the men who had brought her. 'The Soviet Embassy...! But this is ridiculous. I was on my way here.'

One of the men shrugged. The other rang for the lift. Both of them went up with her to the fourth floor and both of them escorted her to a door at the end of a passage. The man who had shrugged went through alone. Varya could hear him speaking to someone. Presently he emerged and motioned to her to go in. She went in quickly, angrily.

There were two men in the room. One had a shaved head and a thick, short neck. He was seated behind a large, flat-topped desk on which there was a blotter, a telephone and a tape recorder. The other, younger and bearded, was standing a little behind him.

The man at the desk said, 'You are Varvara Mikhailovna Lermontov.' It was a statement rather than a question.

Varya nodded impatiently. 'Someone must be crazy. I was already coming here when two idiots snatched me into a car. What is the idea? And who are you?'

'I am a K.G.B. officer from Moscow, citizeness. My name is Tolchik. My colleague here is named Umansky. We have some matters to discuss with you. Please take off your rucksack and sit down.' He pointed to a straight-backed chair on the opposite side of the desk.

Varya glared at him. 'Why "citizeness"? I am accustomed to being called "comrade".'

'"Comrade" is a form of address that has to be earned,' Tolchik said. 'And it has to *continue* to be earned.'

'I have done nothing to lose the right of it.'

'That remains to be seen. Please be seated.'

Varya took off her pack and put it on the floor by the chair. She was sweating – as much from heat as from apprehension. There was a big radiator near the window and the room was stifling. She unzipped her quilted jacket, and sat down. 'Now will you kindly tell me what all this is about?'

Tolchik leaned back. 'Two days ago,' he

said, 'some remnants of the aeroplane you and your fellow-climbers were sent to locate were found at the foot of the mountain on the Soviet side. There were signs that an explosion had occurred. Among the bits of debris picked up were fragments of the camera you were told to retrieve. Worthless fragments. It seems, therefore, that our enemies succeeded in fulfilling their mission – and that you failed to fulfil yours.'

'Yes,' Varya said. 'I am sorry, but it is so.'

Tolchik switched on the tape recorder. 'I would like to have your account of everything that happened on the mountain. In detail, please.'

Varya started on her story. She described the ascent of her party, the collapse of the cornice, the encounter with Royce and Brogan, the explosion and the avalanche, the death of Brogan, the continued bad weather, and her decision to climb down with Royce. She paused only once in her long recital, while Tolchik turned over the tape.

There was a little silence after she'd finished. Then Tolchik said, 'You assumed, did you, that your two comrades were killed at once when the cornice collapsed?'

'I am sure they were.'

'If, by some chance, they had merely been buried in snow and not killed, and you had been able to rescue them, your mission might after all have been fulfilled?'

'Perhaps,' Varya said. 'But any attempt at rescue was out of the question. There was thick cloud over the mountain, and darkness had fallen. No one could have done anything.'

'So – if they *were* still alive – you left them to die.'

'I had no choice. I tell you it was impossible to reach them.'

'Is it not the duty of a Master of Sport to attempt even the impossible when the lives of her climbing companions are at stake?'

'Not in those circumstances. It would have been suicide.'

'And you were not willing to risk your life?'

'It would have been to no purpose. I know what the situation was – and you do not. I resent very much the suggestion you are making.'

'Your protest is on record, citizeness... Now let us turn to the events of the following day, when the American Brogan destroyed the camera. You knew, of course, how vital the recovery of this instrument was to your country. You were informed of this before you left Moscow. What steps did you take to try and prevent its destruction?'

'What steps could I take?' Varya said. 'I was a woman on my own, against two men.'

'A woman with the will to intervene might well have thought of something... I understand you to say that to reach the camera Brogan had to climb down on a rope.'

'That is so.'

'And you were sitting close by, watching?'

'I was watching because there was nothing else I could do.'

'You were not tied up? You were not a prisoner?'

'No.'

'Royce's attention was very much concentrated on Brogan, no doubt?'

'Well – yes.'

'I believe you said he actually moved away from where the rope was fixed, in order to obtain a better view of the descent?'

'Yes.'

'And you had an ice axe... If you had suddenly attacked the rope with your axe, and cut it, would Brogan not have fallen?'

Varya looked at him in horror. 'Cut the rope...! I am not a murderess. You must be out of your mind.'

'*Could* you have cut it?'

'Perhaps. But...'

'If you had done so, the camera would not have been destroyed.'

'It never occurred to me. How could I cut the rope of a fellow climber? It is unthinkable.'

'Brogan was invading Soviet territory. He was engaging in an act hostile to your country. On the soil of your country.'

'Yes... Even so, I could not have cut the rope.'

'What you are saying, citizenness, is that you allowed sentiment to stand in the way of your duty... Sentiment – or worse.'

'What do you mean – *worse?*'

'I am coming to that,' Tolchik said. 'Why did you descend the mountain on the Turkish side? Why did you not wait for the helicopter to come and pick you up, as was arranged?'

'I told you why not. The weather was bad, and I had no food.'

'The weather improved the day you began to descend. Why were you in such a hurry?'

'I could not know that the weather would improve.'

'You could have waited for a day, to see. Even without food, you could have waited for a day.'

'If the weather had remained bad, I would have died.'

'You preferred to leave the Soviet Union, rather than take that chance?'

'I did not want to leave. But I did not want to die. I knew we had to descend together. Royce would not go with me – so I had to come with him.'

'You allowed him to impose his will on you.'

'One of us had to give way.'

'And it was you.'

'Yes...'

Tolchik nodded. 'Tell me – what were your relations with this man Royce?'

'Relations? I do not understand you.'

'You knew he was the famous climber?'

'Yes.'

'No doubt you admired him.'

'As a climber, naturally I admired him.'

'Where did you spend the night, citizenness, when you and he were alone on the summit?'

For a moment, Varya hesitated. Then she shrugged. 'I shared his tent,' she said. 'I had already had one night in the snow without shelter. It was very cold.'

'But in the tent it was far from cold... No doubt he made you his mistress?'

Varya looked at Tolchik with contempt. 'If you were a climber, and not a policeman, you would know that you are talking nonsense. You are a stupid fool.'

Tolchik switched off the tape recorder, got up from his chair, walked round the desk to Varya, and slapped her hard across the face. 'Control your tongue, citizeness – or you will find yourself in even worse trouble than you are in already.' He walked back to his seat, and switched on the recorder again.

Varya, her hand to her face, stared at him disbelievingly.

'Now I will repeat,' Tolchik said. 'He made you his mistress.'

218

'No.'

'He did not make love to you at all?'

'*No!*'

'At least you will admit that on your way down the mountain your relations were very close?'

'We were close as all climbers on a rope are close. We knew we would live or die together. What can be closer?'

'There was nothing more than that?'

'Nothing.'

Tolchik exchanged glances with his silent colleague. Umansky took something from his pocket and gave it to Tolchik. Tolchik said, 'This is a photograph, citizeness, taken through a telescopic lens two days ago from one of our helicopters.' He passed it across the table.

Varya looked at the picture. The exposure had been made in a poor light, but the detail was plain enough. It showed herself and Royce lying together on the mountain ledge, facing each other and locked in a close embrace.

'Well?' Tolchik said. 'Would you describe that relationship as a platonic one?'

Dismayed, Varya passed the photograph back. 'I knew nothing of it. The night was very cold. In our sleep, we must have moved together for warmth. There was no more to it than that.'

Tolchik shook his head. 'You are not

telling the truth... Do you deny that you are in love with William Royce?'

'No,' Varya said, 'I do not deny that. I am deeply in love with him... But nothing has happened between us. And nothing will happen. To-day, I said good-bye to him, and left him.'

'You left him, certainly – but for how long? Were you not in fact going to keep another appointment with him?'

'I do not understand you.'

'Yesterday afternoon, citizeness, an employee of ours who is stationed at the Kars Palace Hotel intercepted a telephone conversation between William Royce and a mountaineering friend of his named Everett. Royce mentioned to his friend the possibility that he might marry a girl he had just met. He discussed with his friend the possibility of a short delay in Ankara so that, if the girl were willing, the marriage could take place. He also discussed the possibility of the girl accompanying the two of them to India.'

'I knew nothing of this,' Varya said.

Tolchik gave a sour smile. 'Perhaps not at the time – but I suggest that by this morning you knew everything. I suggest that the final arrangement was made between you and Royce last night when you dined with him in borrowed clothes and danced with him so lovingly and afterwards went driving with him. I suggest that you agreed to marry him and go with him to India, and that this morning you were on your way to his hotel, where he would join you.'

'It is not so. I have told you. I was on my way here.'

'The information I have is different,' Tolchik said. 'When the car picked you up, you were walking *away* from here... You were walking in the direction of the hotel.'

'I had missed the turning. It was an accident.'

'For you,' Tolchik said, 'it will prove to have been a most unfortunate accident...' His tone became harsher. 'In the light of all the circumstances, the position is only too clear. You are not, as you have pretended to be, a loyal citizen of the Soviet Union. When you climbed the mountain, the wish to defect was already in your mind. That is why you did not attempt to help your companions. That is why you allowed the camera to be destroyed. That is why you seized your opportunity to descend the mountain on this side. That is why you agreed to go with Royce to the British Embassy, instead of coming here at once to report on your mission. That is why you allowed yourself to fall in love with him. That is why you were planning to marry him and go with him to India – because you are a deserter, a defector, a traitor to your country.'

'It is not true,' Varya cried. 'What you are

saying is lies. All of it is lies...'

Tolchik pushed back his chair. 'At two o'clock this afternoon,' he said, 'a plane will be arriving to take you back to Moscow. There you will answer in full for your behaviour. You may recall that under article 64 of the Soviet Criminal Code, the penalty for emigrating without permission is a minimum of ten years' imprisonment, or death... Until this afternoon, you will remain in this room. If you give the slightest trouble, a sedative will be administered to you.'

He picked up the tape recorder and motioned to his colleague. Together, they left the room. As the door closed behind them, there was the sound of a key turning in the lock.

Varya, her mind in turmoil, sat staring at the floor.

She sat there for fifteen minutes, without moving. Then she got up and went to the window.

It was a French window, a double one, with inside and outside pairs of doors and a foot-wide space between them. Beyond it there was a protective iron balcony. The cracks around the doors, she saw, had been sealed with tape against the winter cold. She started to scrape off the tape with her finger nails. In a few minutes she had freed one of the inner doors. Slowly and carefully, she pressed

222

down the handle and pulled. For a moment she thought the door must be locked. She pulled a little harder – and with a squeak of hinges and wood, it flew open. She stood still, her heart pounding, fearful that a guard might have heard. But there was no sound from the passage. She stepped into the space between the doors and scraped the tape off one of the outer ones. That came open more easily. She peered down through the iron railings of the balcony. The room she was in was at the back of the embassy. Below her she could see the garden path she had been hurried along from the gate. Four storeys down. Fifty feet beneath her. And apart from the balcony, the wall was as smooth as an egg. Not a drain pipe in sight. Not another window within reach…

She turned away. Suddenly her glance fell on the rucksack by her chair. *Of course…!* With desperate haste she untied the neck of the sack and pulled out her spare rope. A hundred and twenty feet of it. She carried it to the window, and doubled it, and made the middle of it fast to the balcony railing.

She looked down again. The garden was empty. There was no one in sight… Then, as she prepared to leave, she heard a door open below. A woman's voice called out some-thing in Russian. A shower of tins clattered into a waste bin. The door slammed shut. Out beyond the garden gate a car went slowly by. Then silence. Varya grasped the doubled rope, passed it under her thigh and over her shoulder, and lowered herself backwards over the balcony rail. In twenty seconds she had roped down.

Speed was all that mattered now. She turned and fled. Down the path, out of the gate and along the road. She ran in blind panic, not caring what direction she took, caring only to find human beings, another car, anything. Suddenly she came out into the Boulevard, and there were plenty of people, all staring at her. A taxi cruised by, and she stopped it, and flung herself in. 'The British Embassy,' she gasped.

Royce was in the drive, checking the van tyres for his journey. He looked up at the sound of running feet. '*Varya!*' he cried.

She went to him with hands outstretched. He took her in his arms, incredulously. 'My love…!'

She pressed her face against his shoulder. Tears flowed unchecked down her cheeks. 'Oh, darling – hold me tight…'

'Varya…! What's happened?'

'What you said – an earthquake…!' She brushed away the tears with the sleeve of her jacket, and looked up at him, and tried to smile. 'Oh, I am so thankful to be with you…' Then she started to cry again.